The Strange Garden

Garden

And Other Weird Tales

A Collection of Works by Alex Kingsley

Copyright © 2023 by Alex Kingsley
All rights reserved

Published in the United States by Strong Branch Press, a
division of Strong Branch Productions.

strongbranchproductions.com

This work is fiction. Names, characters, places, and
incidents either are the product of the author's
imagination or are used fictitiously. Any resemblance to
actual persons, living or dead, events, or locales is
coincidental.

ISBN: 9781088092217

Cover design by Ross Setterfield.

alexkingsley.org

For my family. What a bunch of weirdos.

The Strange Garden and Other Weird Tales

A Collection of Works by Alex Kingsley

CONTENTS

Author's Note

Hello. Welcome to this book.

Fair warning: some of these stories are very silly. Others are very disturbing. I know it's not common practice to preface a book with content warnings, but I'd rather break convention than leave some poor reader traumatized. So, if you want to leap into these stories completely unspoiled, then read on, brave soul. If, however, you want to check and see what content each story deals with, here is a list of elements of each story that have the potential to upset some readers:

The Strange Garden: minor body horror
This Is Not a Place of Honor: isolation, abduction, suicide
Summer Reading Champion: mind control
Steve Goes Home: death, isolation
What I Wouldn't Do for Annie: sexual harassment, body horror, death
His Name Is Chad: death, reference to sexual assault
The Good and Benevolent Reign of Big Ted: euthanasia
Little Acid Girl: harassment, body horror
Dev Fielding and the Call of the In Between: death, suicide, loss of autonomy

The Strange Garden

Originally published in Sci-Fi Lampoon

The wrong mail was delivered to my apartment one day, and I think it really all just spiraled from there. Even though I don't receive much of anything other than bills, advertisements, overdue notices for my bills, and if I'm lucky, one of those neat coupon books, I still make a habit of checking my mailbox every day. One morning, after a lengthy tussle with my mailbox door, I found something unfamiliar inside: a *magazine.* I've never exactly been financially stable enough to have a whole magazine subscription, but I've often wondered what kind of magazine I would subscribe to if I could. Maybe a fashion magazine — but for most of my life I've been a sweatpants-and-sweatshirt kind of person. Perhaps a science magazine — though chances are I wouldn't read any of the issues, and they'd just stack up by my toilet.

But *this* magazine was something I would never have thought to order for myself; It was called *Outdoors Weekly*, and on the glossy cover was a photo of a smiling old lady kneeling in a garden holding a flower pot. It was a little unclear if she was planting things in the pot or if she was planting things from the pot in the ground, but the mystery of it all intrigued me. Who was this woman, and what wisdom did she hold? What was it about her garden that was making her smile? What secrets were hiding behind those eyes? Maybe this was a sign. A sign that I had been stuck in my humdrum ways for too long. I had been Elanor the unemployed artist for years; now I could be Elanor the *gardener*.

I flipped it over and saw that it was meant for my neighbor, but surely they wouldn't miss one issue, would they? So I took it up to my apartment to peruse, flipping through the magazine and enjoying the luxurious smoothness of the pages on my fingers as I idly dreamed that I could be as happy as the flower pot lady on the cover. Then one of the spreads caught my eye. The image showed a group of people, parents and kids and old folks and young people, all sitting at a picnic bench and laughing, and above them in bold white letters were the words: The Power of Community Gardening. Of course! A *community* garden! Why hadn't I thought of it earlier? I could practically see myself in that picture, seated at the picnic table — no, seated *on* the picnic table, because I'd be the cool rebellious one — telling a joke that made the whole group laugh. I imagined myself appearing at the community garden on a sunny summer morning, well-worn straw hat shielding my eyes from the glare, and everyone at the garden says, "Hey, who's that girl? She's new!" And they're all impressed with how quickly I can weed the beds and how tenderly I transplant the tomatoes. Pretty soon I become the celebrity of the community garden. A newcomer joins the ranks of community gardeners. She says, "Hey, who's that girl watering the pumpkin patch?" and one of the senior members laughs and says, "Oh, that's Elanor. You'll want to get to know *her*."

I'd made up my mind: This was my future.

Now the last thing I wanted was to show up and seem like an inexperienced gardener. I mean, I was, but I didn't want anyone to know that. This was a community garden, after all. Probably the whole community would be there. So I looked up a bunch of stock photos of gardeners and tried my best to put together an outfit that said, "I'm a gardener, but I'm not trying too hard to look like one." I bought a straw hat online, but it looked so new when it arrived that I was afraid people would be like, "Hey, did you buy that online?" so I went outside and rubbed some dirt on it. I splurged on a whole set of spades and hoes and banged them on rocks until it looked like I'd been using them for years. I bought a pair of overalls and cut some holes in them to make it look like I'd been wearing them while doing some difficult garden work. I am now realizing that impulsive purchases like this may be the reason I never have enough money for a magazine subscription.

After a bit of research, I discovered that there was a community garden not too far from my new place. Fully outfitted as the gardener that I wasn't, I showed up to find the place deserted. The fence was choked with climbing vines, and I could hardly see into the garden because of all the tall leafy stalks that grew inside. As I approached, I began to lose hope. I peered through the overgrown fence and saw that the inside of the garden was completely deserted. Beyond the weeds, all I could see were empty beds with nothing to boast but dirt. I sighed, looking down at my spade forlornly.

Alright, I'd change my dream. Instead of becoming the community garden's most beloved new member, I'd be its only member. I'd build this garden from the ground up, and when people passed by me working they'd say, "Hey, I love your garden!" and I'd say "Actually, it's the community garden," and they'd walk away thinking about what a cool and selfless person I was to be working in the community garden. And then the next day a pretty girl shows up to work at the garden with me, and she doesn't share my gardening expertise, but she's eager to help. I teach her everything I know about gardening, which at that point is a lot, and together we weed and plant seeds and do all those other things that gardeners do. And the whole time we're smiling at each other then looking away then smiling again then looking away. Then when we're harvesting the zucchini, our hands touch. And then —

I heard a crash so loud I almost screamed. Actually I did scream. I lied because I was embarrassed. But yeah, I screamed. I'm not sure if I said words, but it was something along the lines of "Hecking fuck!"

"Sorry to scare you, dear," said a quavering voice, and I whirled around to see a stout old lady peering out of a dilapidated wooden shed. "I seemed to have knocked down a few shovels. Silly old me!"

This was my moment! My time to make community friends at the community garden! But instead of showing the old woman what a charismatic and charming person I am, I simply stared at her with my mouth hanging open, beginning to tremble as my social anxiety set in.

The woman waddled out of the shed, and I could see her better in the sunlight. Her long grey hair was twisted into two haphazard braids, which danced across her faded floral dress. Her thick brown work boots looked out of place against the wispy pink fabric. She dusted off her gloved hands and held one out for me to shake.

"My name's Francine," she grinned, showing off her yellowing teeth. I shook her hand and smiled, forgetting that introducing myself was a key part of social interactions.

"And you are?" she prompted.

"Oh! Right! Yes!" I stammered. "I'm Elanor!"

"And have you come to work in the community garden, Elanor?"

"Yes I have!" I confirmed, probably puffing up my chest with pride a little too much, and maybe even subconsciously pointing to my hat.

"I am just so thankful to see young people taking an interest in gardening," she said, hobbling over to the shed. "Let me just get you started. There are some empty beds over there you can work on." She waved her hand vaguely to the whole garden. She disappeared into the shed for a moment, and I heard some rustling. When she reappeared, she held something cupped in her hands.

"Here, take some of my special seeds." She took my hands and clasped them in hers, and I felt a few hard little pellets fall into my palm. When she took her hand away, I brought the seeds up to my face and — okay, this is when things get a little weird. There's not — okay I'm just gonna say it. The things she put in my hand were not seeds. They were human teeth.

I'm not sure what a normal person would have done in that situation. Maybe say, "Hey, these are human teeth!" But I am not a normal person. I get nervous. This little old lady was probably just confused. Maybe she was going senile? Maybe she had accidentally switched her dentures with the seeds? No, that's not right. Dentures don't come as individual teeth. Still, what could I do? Well, I know exactly what I could have done. I could have turned around and left the moment there were teeth in my hands. I could have said "Ma'am, these are not seeds, and you are not a very good gardener!" But I didn't. I simply smiled and said, "Thank you, Francine," and went to one of the beds where she had directed me.

I spent three hours there. Three hours of smiling and nodding as Francine told me about what had happened on last night's reruns of *The Golden Girls* while I buried teeth two inches below the ground because, according to Francine, "that's what it said to do on the back of the packet." And the weird part was? I actually enjoyed it. She asked me a few questions, like "Where are you from?" and "What's your job?" and "Oh why are you having such a hard time finding a job?" and "Well, are you at least finding friends?" and "Why do you have such a hard time making friends?" and "Are you crying?" Normal small talk stuff like that. It was nice just to have someone ask questions about me for once, and to feel like I was a part of something, even if that something I was a part of was a garden run by a crazy old lady who planted teeth instead of seeds.

I wish I could say the story ends there. But it doesn't.

Because the next day I wanted to go back. I thought, hey, that was a little weird, but ya know what? Francine is probably really desperate for the company. I owe it to *her* to go back again. So I put on a new set of gardening clothes, complete with my trusty hat, and I ventured back to the garden.

"Oh, Elanor! I am so delighted to see you!" Francine clapped her frail little hands when she saw me approaching. "And back so soon, too!"

I blushed a little, hoping she didn't know that I was here because I didn't have anywhere else to go.

"I just love community gardening so much," I said, and before I could stop myself, "Besides, I have nowhere else to go." Damn it! I wasn't supposed to say that part!

"Yesterday's plants are doing quite nicely!" she cooed.

"That's great!" I responded instinctively, before remembering that yesterday's plants were teeth. I felt my smile falter. "They are?" I asked.

"Have a look!" Francine pointed towards the beds where I had been planting, and I went to kneel down next to them. Sure enough, where I'd buried each of the teeth, little green leaves were pushing their way out of the soil. I stared at the buds in disbelief. Had I been wrong about the whole teeth thing? Had I actually been planting teeth-shaped seeds, and I was just being ageist for ever assuming that this old lady could get seeds and teeth confused? Can seeds even germinate that fast? I was about to ask Francine this, then remembered that I really didn't want her to know that I wasn't a super experienced gardener. So I simply said, "They look healthy!" because that seemed like an appropriate plant descriptor.

"They are!" Francine said from where she stood at the gate of the garden, "*very* healthy. So you wouldn't mind doing a little more planting for me this afternoon? I would do it myself, but my back —"

"Of course!" I cut in. The last thing I wanted to do was bury more teeth, but I couldn't say no to an old lady with back problems.

"Wonderful," Francine's face crinkled with delight, and she hobbled over to the shed.

"What will you be having me plant today?" I asked innocently, hoping she would say something like cucumbers or carrots.

"I've got another set of seeds somewhere in here," she answered unhelpfully from the shed. "Ah! Here we are!"

She plopped into my hands what appeared to be a giant clump of human hair.

"Is this...is this one seed?" I asked tentatively.

"No, no, it's many! You sort of disperse them, you know? Like lettuce seeds."

"Right. Yes. Like lettuce." I couldn't let her know that I didn't know how to plant lettuce seeds.

"And what..." I ventured, "what will this grow?"

Again Francine grinned in such a way that made her yellow smile look like a thick crescent moon. "A beautiful flower," she answered, and her voice dripped with so much sweetness I almost ached to see what that flower would look like when it was grown. Besides, I was a little comforted. I knew what I was planting: flowers. I was planting flowers. With...with hair-shaped seeds. But this is also what lettuce seeds are like, so clearly it can't be too weird. Right?

I shouldn't have gone back to the garden. I know I shouldn't have gone back. But I woke up the next morning, and I thought, "Elanor, what are you going to do today?" and I had no response. Zero ideas. Nothing. So I put on my hat, and I went to the garden.

Sure enough, Francine was waiting there for me.

"Back again, I see," she grinned.

"Yeah, well, ya know..."

By "ya know" I meant, "I have an insatiable passion for community gardening," but instead Francine guessed, "Lonely with nothing to do?"

"Uh," I shuffled my feet, "Yeah."

"Well, I'll have something for you to do," Francine volunteered, pointing zealously over to the plot where I'd dispersed the hair and — well, it really shouldn't have surprised me at this point, but it still did. The previous day that bed was nothing but empty dirt. Now it was a line of little green stalks, each protruding about a foot above the ground, and at the top of each was a blushing pink flower. I felt the magnetic pull of those flowers, and I walked past the gate and into the garden without so much as glancing at Francine.

The petals were smooth and soft, and they cascaded away from the center of the flower like little peach waterfalls with streaks of crimson. In the middle of the flower was a hard white spike. Was that normal for a flower? I couldn't say, because looking at that flower I felt like I had never seen another flower in my life. I knelt by each in turn and examined them. They were all different shades — some were such a pale pink that they looked almost white, and others were closer to brown or black, but they all shared the same bright red streaks and stiff white center. I rubbed the petals between my fingers, and they almost felt warm.

"Aren't they lovely?" I finally heard Francine say behind me.

"Yes," I murmured, as if in a trance. "What kind of flowers are they?"

"The Blossom of Man's Sins."

"What?" I turned around to look at her, as I'd expected her to just say "zinnias" or something like that.

Francine shrugged. "I just call them 'sin flowers' though. The whole name is kind of a mouthful."

"Is that…" I glanced back and forth between the woman and the flowers, "is that like a normal kind of flower? Like azaleas or something?"

She smiled. "Kind of like azaleas. Yes. But full of sin."

"Huh. Okay." I stood up, brushing off the dirt from my pants. "So is sin, like…is that a special kind of fertilizer?"

Francine cackled, and her long braids swung back and forth. "You could say that," she said coyly, which really bothered me because if it *was* some kind of fertilizer, as a gardener-in-training, I needed to know that kind of information. I didn't want to seem too desperate though, so I nodded as if to say, "right, yes, I knew that."

"So…do you want me to plant something else?" I ventured.

"Oh no!" Francine pressed her fingertips together, "today I have a very special task for you. It's the harvest!"

"The harvest?" I didn't know much about agriculture, but I was fairly certain that you couldn't harvest anything that had only been planted two days ago. Nevertheless, she gestured over to the bed where I planted the maybe-teeth, and I saw that where yesterday there were only little buds, today there was a whole line of bushes. The leaves were lush and green, and hanging down from the branches were little red fruits.

"I...um..." I stammered, because this time I was really sure something was wrong, but I didn't want to get called out for my lack of agricultural knowledge.

"Try one," Francine whispered, suddenly behind me, placing a hand on my shoulder. "Try one, Elanor. Try one. They are delicious."

Listen, I grew up as the kind of kid who was constantly eating berries I found and then getting yelled at by my parents because those weren't berries those were actually just mothballs and how could I be so stupid, I was already ten years old, and I was still eating things I found and wasn't I smarter than this? So at this point I was pretty well trained not to eat random fruit that I stumbled upon. Still, the bulbous red fruits looked so encouraging, so engorged with crimson juice. It was like the opposite of Adam and Eve. Like it would be a sin *not* to eat the fruit.

I slowly reached out and plucked one of the fruits from the branch. It caved in a little at my touch, like a water balloon that was not quite filled to bursting, but if I pressed it, it would pop. What kind of plant was this? I had no idea. In truth, I didn't understand any of the work I had been doing. As I looked down at the ripe fruit in my hand, I felt the sinking sensation of unworthiness. A lump rose in my throat as hot tears burned in my eyes. I dropped the fruit, and I heard it splatter on the dirt, spraying red juice everywhere.

"I'm sorry," I sobbed, "I don't deserve to eat any of the fruits. I don't know what I'm doing. I don't even know what kind of plant that is. I've never heard of a sin flower. I've never been to a community garden before. I rubbed dirt on this hat. See, look. I put that dirt there. I'm an imposter. I'm a fraud. I'm so sorry. I'll just go."

I ran for the gate, but Francine's voice stopped me.

"I know, sweetheart."

I froze, one hand already on the chain link. "You do?" I sniffled.

"Of course. If you knew anything about gardens, anything at all, you probably would have stopped working here as soon as I gave you the Flesh Berry seeds."

"You mean you knew — sorry, the what?"

"Honey, no one in their right mind would stay at a garden like this, so I knew right away that you had serious issues."

"Is this...is this not a normal garden?"

Francine shook her head ruefully, and her braids danced. "No, Elanor. This is a very strange garden."

"Is that...is that why there's no one else here but you?"

Francine laughed. "No! That's because when someone comes to work here, I kill them."

I blinked. "You...you kill them?"

"Of course I do. Where do you think I get all the teeth and hair from?"

"So those were teeth!" I shouted victoriously. "I thought maybe — wait, I'm sorry, could we go back to the part where you kill people?"

"People volunteer to work the garden. And I kill them," Francine explained as though it were the most natural thing in the world. "But don't you worry! Not a single part of them goes to waste. I keep 'em right in the shed over there, and I use every part of them as seeds. Everything from their pinky toes to their hopes for the future. It all goes into the garden."

I wrung my hands together, glancing over to the shed.

"So...why didn't you kill me?" I asked.

"Honestly?" Francine fixed me with a condescending gaze. "You just seemed kind of pathetic."

"Wait," I held up a hand, "You're telling me that you didn't kill me because my life was too *sad*?"

"Sweetheart, you rubbed dirt on your straw hat to try to fit in."

"Did...did it work?"

"No honey. No it didn't." I felt hot indignation rising in my chest.

"So I wasn't *good enough* for you to kill?" I fumed.

Francine shook her head. "It's not like that, angel. You simply haven't sinned enough for me to ever grow a sin flower out of your hair. And you certainly haven't lived enough life to grow a decent Flesh Berry."

"Well fine!" I exclaimed. "Maybe I'll go to another community garden, and they'd be happy to plant my hair!"

Francine shook her head in defeat once again. "You're a strange one, Elanor. I'll give you that. You are a strange one." She turned her back on me and waddled back into her shed, which I now knew was full of corpses of community gardeners. I put my straw hat back on my head and collected as many Flesh Berries as I could before leaving, hoping to prove that I *wasn't* so pathetic after all. That night I tried chopping them up and putting them in a salad, but I had to throw the whole thing away because they made the salad taste like blood. I cried for an hour, and then I decided to check and see if there was another community garden near me. The closest one was an hour's drive away, but I figured it was worth it.

At the next community garden, they gave me weird looks when I tried planting my hair. A girl named Georgia told me that I needed to use actual seeds, like from a pouch. And when she gave me the actual seeds, they didn't look like human teeth at all. She looked a little confused when I commented on this, but she didn't say anything. She taught me everything she knew about gardening, which was a lot. She showed me how to plant cucumbers below a trellis, and how to pluck the basil flowers when the plant starts to bolt. We weeded and planted seeds and did all those other things that gardeners do. And the whole time we were smiling at each other and looking away and then smiling at each other then looking away.

And then when we were harvesting the zucchini, our hands touched.

This Is Not a Place of Honor

Originally published in Radon Journal

I had been locked in my cement palace for two thousand three hundred forty-seven years and one hundred thirty-eight days when I heard the knocking. There had never been knocking before. The people on the surface do not dare come near my home.

I bounded up the stairs, metallic clanks echoing with each step, and threw open the outside door. Before me was a barren wasteland, the soil long turned to parched sand. There were no trees, only the black spikes that protruded from the ground in the area surrounding my door, warning travelers not to come near. And for the most part, these warnings worked. People feared the land where even the ground itself was hostile, and they kept their distance. Until today.

Standing a few paces away was a little boy. His face was smeared with dirt and painted with scratches. He wore rags that were haphazardly cut to be clothing. His dark hair was matted and caked with mud. A cut on his knee leaked blood down his shin onto his makeshift shoes, once plastic water bottles. He looked up at me with the innocent eyes of a child who does not know what kind of danger he is staring in the face. He was dwarfed by the massive black spikes jutting out from the red ground.

"Excuse me," he said, "but have you seen my cat?" He spoke in a language that was not English, but had once been English, until the millennia had twisted it and morphed it into something entirely different. I no longer find things beautiful, but if I could, I would find the evolution of language beautiful, I think. I was created to predict the many ways that language would shift over time, so after a moment of processing I was able to comprehend unhampered.

And then, of course, came the chorus of inner voices. It was usually only a whisper in my head, but here he was! A real child! My purpose ready to be fulfilled! And the words that usually came in a whisper now came in a scream.

Speak the words. Speak them.

But it had been so long since I'd spoken to anyone. Surely I could savor this moment just a little longer?

"Yes," I lied. To tell an untruth caused my insides to fry.

Disobedient. Speak the words.

"I have seen your cat." I pressed on, despite the searing in my mind, the flashing warnings in my eyes. "I brought him inside. Would you like to come in?"

It had been so long. One visitor could do no harm.

This is not the protocol. Speak the words.

The child glanced at me quizzically, taking in my physical form. I must have looked so strange to him, my clothes untouched by the elements, my coat a pristine white, my face a near-human approximation of what it once was. Perhaps he was considering if I was a danger, or perhaps if I was a god. I think I am both.

After a moment of thought he nodded, rubbing some of the dirt from his face. He followed me into the darkness of the doorway where we stood and peered down the steps behind me.

"It's dark," he said.

"I do not need light," I told him. "But I can put some on for you."

At my command, the lights flickered on. They had not been used for many years. Seeing how deep the stairs reached into the earth, the child instinctively reached for my hand.

"Your hand is cold," the child said.

"Yes."

"Do you feel cold?"

"No."

"Your skin is hard."

"Yes."

"Why?"

"Shall we go downstairs?"

The boy nodded, and together we descended.

It was a concrete prison, with long, empty halls that I walked through day in and day out, no sound but the metallic echo of my footsteps. No company but the words, the words that repeat themselves in my mind, a whisper from another time. And still, I am damned to this place for all of eternity.

I know exactly how long I've rotted away in the confines of the stone labyrinth. Except I do not rot. I look exactly the same as I did when they left me here. But inside, something has changed. I am not the person I used to be — the words, they've infected me, turned me into something else. And all the while I see the clock tick-ticking in my mind, as the world deteriorates and dies and then is reborn, and civilization forgets and rediscovers what it once was, and the Earth moves and moves and moves, I stay the same.

I enjoyed the child's warmth, the simple warmth of a human being by my side once again. He did not ask any questions on the way down, but I could feel him begin to tremble.

"Do not fear, little one," I said. "We are almost there."

At the base of the steps, I commanded more lights to turn on. For the first time in many years, my home was illuminated, the concrete halls bathed in a blue fluorescent glow.

"Where is your bed?" the boy asked.

"I need no bed. I do not sleep."

"Don't you get tired?"

"Yes. I am very tired. But I do not get sleepy."

Tell him. Tell him. Tell him.

But I did not. It had been so long.

"Where is my cat?" he asked. I gestured forward and led him deeper into the bowels of the tunnels that were my home.

"Why do you live here?" he wondered.

I froze. I did not know how to answer this question.

"Do you know what a *scientist* is?" I could come up with no suitable translation in his language.

The child shook his head no.

"A scientist is someone who observes things, then comes up with ideas based on the things they observe."

"I come up with ideas sometimes too," the child said. "Am I a scientist?"

"Perhaps you are," I mused. "But a very little one. I was a very big scientist."

"You don't look that big."

"I was very smart. And I worked with many other scientists who were also very smart. They were my friends."

The boy looked around eagerly. "Are your friends here?"

I shook my head. "No. My friends died a long time ago."

"How did you survive?"

"I didn't. I died too."

The child frowned.

"You're not dead," he observed.

I smiled, which was strange, because I had not smiled for thousands of years. My face creaked imperceptibly with the effort of a movement it had not made in many centuries.

"I was chosen to survive," I explained. "But only a small piece of me. The rest of me has died."

The boy did not understand, but that was all right, because I did not understand either. Perhaps I once understood, when I was human, but that was long ago.

A plan had just hatched in my mind and was now slowly unfurling its wings. If I could just get this child to follow me deep enough, to go far enough down below, then I would be free.

Disobedient. Disobedient. Speak the words.

The child let go of my hand, taking a step back from me. His footsteps echoed in the large chamber.

"Are you...are you a..." he spoke a word in his language that I did not recognize, but I could surmise his meaning. One who is lost. *Are you a ghost?*

I cannot laugh, but perhaps I would have if I could. Perhaps in a way, I was a ghost. But I could not risk letting the child go, not now that my scheme was beginning to unfold.

"No, little one. I am real. See?" I held out a hand for him to touch once again. Tentatively, he took it.

"But you are cold," he said, "and I am warm."

"My friends," I told him, "they were very smart. And they found a way to turn me into something else. So that I may never die."

"But why?"

Tell him. You must protect him. You must protect all people. It is your duty. It is your only objective.

And thus the words spilled in a deluge, the words that had been clanking around in my metal brain for millennia.

"**This is not a place of honor**," I quoted. "**This is no memorial, nor is it a site of worship. Here you will find nothing of use.**"

I could hear the echo of my voice in the stone chambers, fluttering around like a bird caged for years finally set free.

"**What is here is dangerous and repulsive. I am here to warn you of that danger.**"

"What . . .what is the danger?" the child asked, still holding my metal hand.

"**The danger is present now as it was long ago**," I continued. "**The danger is sleeping, but will wake if disturbed. The danger cannot be seen, but will kill you.**"

"Is my kitty okay?"

"**I am immune to this danger, and I am here to tell you to leave me as its sole guardian. Leave this place and tell others never to return.**"

And with that, for the first moment in over two thousand years, the words ceased.

I do not have many feelings anymore, but when I spoke the words there was a sense of satisfaction, like a rat in a cage pressing the correct lever for the juice reward. I had achieved my purpose, and for that my circuits rewarded me with pleasant firings to let me know it was a job well done.

The boy simply stared at me blankly.

"Can I see my cat now?" he asked.

Send him away. You have spoken the words. Now make him leave.

But my plan was already in motion, and I could not let the first human to step into my home after millennia leave so easily.

"Your cat is in my special room," I said. "Will you follow me?"

The child nodded, and allowed me to lead him deeper down into the earth.

With each step the pain became worse. The residual pleasure of speaking the words had faded, and now all I could feel was the burn of my circuits attempting to punish me for my transgression. My vision flashed with bright red warnings.

Turn back. Turn back. Turn back.

But I did not want to turn back.

As we walked down the corridor, I saw the boy's eyes flicking around the place in amazement. At one point they landed on a large metal slab, and I could tell he was attempting to understand the ancient symbols. However, his own tongue was now so distant from the English that it was birthed from, I knew those letters must have looked like nothing more than meaningless squiggles. I, on the other hand, was all too familiar with the sign drilled to that metal wall:

CAUTION! NUCLEAR WASTE BELOW!

We arrived at a metal door, only slightly rusted from the years that it had weathered. I pulled the handle, and it creaked open.

"Come," I said, and led the child into the pitch darkness, closing the door behind us. Only once we were both securely in the room did I command the lights on.

"My kitty is not in here," the child observed, and I could hear panic tinge his voice.

"There is something better," I said, indicating the humming box that was fit snugly into its own cement alcove. "There is a magic box."

His eyes widened. "Why is it magic?"

I strode over to the box and flipped open the little plastic cover that concealed a small black button. Flashing warnings strobed inside my eyes. I ignored them.

"If you press that button," I said levelly, "I will finally be able to sleep."

"But you said you do not sleep," the boy remembered.

"I do not. So you can imagine how nice it might be for me to finally sleep after all this time."

Warning: this will shut down your power supply. You will not recharge. This will terminate your program.

Yes, I silently told the voice buzzing in my metal brain, I am aware.

Warning: the facility will go into lockdown. The child will be trapped.

And how lovely it will be, I thought, to have human company in my dying moments.

"Press the button, child, and I will bring you to your cat."

The boy rubbed some more of the dirt from his face, considering this offer. Then, like the docile little child he was, nodded.

"Very good. This button. Right here."

He lifted his tiny hand up to the button. He was barely tall enough to reach it.

"Thank you, little one," I said as his finger hovered over the button. If I were still able to cry, I would have. "Thank you."

A delicate mew echoed through the chamber.

"My kitty!" the boy squealed. He ran towards the door, forgetting to press the button. Throwing it open, he saw waiting in the hallway was a black and white cat, with one torn ear and a missing eye, calling for its companion.

I must have left the front entrance open. I never thought to shut the door.

The little boy scooped the creature up in his arms.

"Thank you, scientist!" The boy said it cheerfully before making his hasty departure. As he left, I could hear his voice echoing against the cement: "I hope you get to sleep soon!"

The red flashing stopped. The voice went back to a whisper. I could still hear the child's footsteps echoing in the cavernous hallways as he made his ascent back to the surface, leaving me alone in the depths.

I won't, little one, I thought. I will never sleep again.

Summer Reading Champion

Originally published in The Storage Papers

The guidance counselor told me that it wasn't too late for me to get on the right track. Which I thought was stupid, honestly — the idea that there was a "right track" and a "wrong track" for me.

"You're only a sophomore," she told me. "There's still time to make up for your mistakes."

I guess there's no use hiding it. I mean, it feels weird to admit to the police that you were selling pot out of the second floor girl's bathroom every third period after Mr. Thompson's class ended, but then again, you guys already busted me for that, so you know that part already. The thing is, I didn't think of it so much as a "mistake." High schoolers are stressed. They need something to help them chill. Thanks to my big brother, I had that something, and I didn't really think there was anything wrong with that.

I didn't say this to the guidance counselor, though. I just told her that I didn't think colleges would look fondly upon a fifteen-year-old who'd already racked up a criminal charge. She laughed, and I remember the way her beaded glasses chain waggled, she told me that I was not the first weed dealer she'd helped to get into college.

"Colleges love to see that you're engaging in your community," she told me, "and since you're still relatively young, if you get started now and stick with it, it'll really look like you're committed to whatever activity you pick."

I tried not to laugh. First of all, I'm pretty sure selling drugs to students was already pretty great community engagement, but colleges wouldn't see it that way. But I guess what really got me was that it all seemed so fake. Pretending that you really like something just so colleges will say, "Oh, that kid's got passion! Oh, that kid's going places!" She shoved a bunch of brochures at me, telling me to "peruse these opportunities for promising youths" and get back to her.

I chucked them as soon as I got home, but my dad found them in the trash.

He told me, "If this is how Mrs. Vale thinks you're getting into college, then goddamnit, you're doing it."

I looked through the brochures, and they all seemed pretty boring. Volunteering at a children's museum. Working at a homeless shelter. Doing paperwork for some environmental nonprofit. I managed to eliminate all of them except one: the city library. It's not that I was exactly thrilled at the possibility of re-shelving books, but I figured it sounded a lot better than spending my day with a bunch of screaming children trying to force them to learn about the life cycle of a bee, so that was the one I picked.

I went on Monday afternoon after school and was greeted like a returning war hero.

"You must be Bailey!" I remember the woman at the front desk clasped her hands together, like my appearance was an answer to her prayers. She took me into a back office, where there was a spindly old man rubbing a wet paper towel on old children's books.

"Welcome, newest addition to the Children's Section!" he said, much to my disappointment. The whole reason I took this job was to get away from a job with kids. Still, there was hope. Maybe they'd just have me preparing arts and crafts. Maybe I wouldn't have to interact with kids at all.

The lanky man introduced himself as Randy, and he rushed me away on a tour of the building. It's funny what constitutes a big landmark in a tiny local library. He was particularly proud of the color copier, which is apparently a coveted thing in the library business.

The big climax of the tour was the Reading Room. I didn't want to be impressed by the library, but to be honest, the Reading Room was pretty cool. The carpet was blood red with little black dots that made me think of a ladybug, and one full wall of the room was covered in huge arched windows, with wooden spokes that reached down to connect at a central hub, like hands on a clock. There were no lights in the room. It was only lit by the sunlight streaming in from the windows. The floor was littered with multicolored pillows, now unoccupied. At the head of the room was a rocking chair with a stack of children's books on the floor nearby it.

"This place is actually pretty nice," I told Randy, and he looked so proud, like he'd built the library himself.

"Why thank you," he said, and took me back downstairs to give me more information about what I'd be doing for my job. A lot of it wasn't so bad — laminating posters, folding brochures, making decorations for the "Book of the Month" display. But every weekend, I was expected to be there for Read Aloud Time. I didn't want to let Randy know this, but I was dreading that part. I do *not* like hanging out with kids, and regardless of how pretty that Reading Room was, I didn't enjoy the prospect of sitting on the multicolored pillows, doing stupid nursery rhymes with a bunch of drooling, sniffling, grimy toddlers. But Randy had this kind of pouty face, one you couldn't say no to, so of course I told him I would be there bright and early Sunday morning.

I was really dragging my feet on my first Sunday, but once I saw all those cute little faces, so eager to hear about Peter Rabbit and Mother Goose or whatever talking animal they were going to learn about today, I felt my heart just melt a little. I remember thinking, "Oh, okay. I can make this work."

Basically my job was just to sit with them and listen to the story while Randy sat in the rocking chair reading.

Read Aloud always started with the Reading Time Song. It wasn't so much a song really as a chant — I think it's too much to ask of little kids to stay in tune. Before the story began, they would speak the words aloud with the accompanying hand gestures. It went like this:

I open my heart
I open my mind
I open a book
And I read what's inside

I keep my hands to myself
And I won't be too loud
So all of my friends
Can enjoy Read Aloud

It was pretty sneaky, teaching the kids the rules like that. It was basically a nice way of saying "sit down and shut up." It worked, though. The kids always paid attention during Read Aloud. And as much as I hate to admit it, I paid pretty close attention too. Some of those kids' books are good, okay?

Sunday mornings became my favorite day of the week. I started getting up early to bring the front desk lady — her name is Laura — a bagel and a coffee. I kinda became a local library celebrity. I think it helped that I was the only person working there under the age of fifty. Oh, and I'm sure the fact that I was unpaid labor didn't hurt either. I'm not gonna lie, I have a hard time getting myself motivated for school. I'm not really that interested in chemistry or history or trig or whatever. For a long time I didn't know what I was interested in. Turns out I'm just interested in making kids laugh.

Randy was particularly excited for me to be there for the Summer Reading Program. It's the time of year that the children's section is busiest because kids are coming in with their reading logs to get their hands stamped and to get a reward for how much they read. It encourages kids to read on their own, Randy told me. And to be quite honest, I was looking forward to it too.

Okay, now I know you're probably tired of hearing all that gushy stuff, but that's where the touchy-feely part of the story ends, because a few months into my job was about when things started to go south. I knew something was wrong when I walked in one Sunday morning and Laura was not her usual chipper self. She still had her hands clasped together like she usually did, but this time she was a little shaky, like she was nervous about something. I gave her the usual bagel and coffee, and she just shook her head. I asked her what was wrong. She leaned over the desk and whispered that Randy was gone.

Before I could ask her what she meant, a man I didn't recognize stepped out from what used to be Randy's office. He was a lot younger than Randy, with full dark hair combed back and thick beard. He wore a suit and a crooked smile, two things you don't usually see on someone who works in a public library. The new man introduced himself as Damion, and he said that he'd been transferred from another branch to be Randy's replacement. I asked where

Randy had gone, and he brushed the question aside, saying it wasn't any of his business. Then he told me I was going to be late for Read Aloud and he hurried upstairs.

Before I followed him, I turned to look at Laura. Her eyes were wide with panic. I asked her if Randy had told her anything about retiring and she said no, he'd never mentioned anything about leaving. She'd tried calling him and there was no answer. She'd also asked around to the other branches to see where Damion had come from, and none of them seemed to know who he was.

Despite Laura's franticness, I wasn't actually that concerned. Mostly just confused. What kind of guy just shows up to take over Read Aloud?

Just as I was about to ask Laura some more questions, I heard my name:

"Bailey."

Without turning around, I knew it was him calling me. His voice felt cold, like ice water dripping down my back. I turned around to face him without thinking about it first.

"You're late for reading time. Come."

"Yes sir," I said reflexively, and followed him upstairs.

That was the first Sunday that we did not do the Read Aloud Song. Damion said he had a new song to teach the kids. It went like this:

We invite him to come in
We invite him to come feast
We invite him to our doorstep

We invite the hungry beast

We give him all he asks for
Anything he needs
We invite him to come in
So that he may feed

Damion didn't teach the kids fun hand gestures like Randy did. He made them cover their faces with their hands as they spoke.

Usually that's when Randy would go on to read the story, but Damion didn't do that. He started handing out sheets of paper. He called them "reading logs" and he said they were part of the Summer Reading Program. Only thing was, they didn't look like the reading logs you usually give to kids — lined pages covered with clipart of books and caterpillars and things like that. These were blank. And instead of instructing them to write the books they read and bring the reading log in to get a stamp and a reward, he told them to write down what they believe in. The child who believed the most would be the Summer Reading Champion.

After Read Aloud, I told him I thought it was a really weird nursery rhyme. He said it was just something he used to do as a little kid, that it was about feeding a stray dog. I told him I still thought it was really weird, and he just glared at me. Usually I have no problem with people looking at me funny, but this was the first glare I ever got that truly made me want to run away. And it was just over his stupid nursery rhyme.

I was hoping maybe there was some mistake, that Damion was a temporary replacement and that Randy would return, but from that day forward, I only saw his crooked little smile when I looked into Randy's office. I wanted to quit, but every time I made my decision that I'd had enough, it was like he knew, and he appeared behind me, asking me to stay. And I didn't want to stay, but somehow I still found myself saying yes.

Laura disappeared. Not in the same way Randy did, luckily. I showed up one day with a bagel and coffee for her and she was gone. I called her and she told me that she just couldn't stand it anymore. Something wasn't right and she didn't want to be there. I was jealous of her, actually. I don't know why I kept coming in, watching the kids do their chant and turn in their "reading logs" every Sunday morning.

I'm not sure what would have happened if I hadn't forgotten my jacket that day. Summer was coming to a close and it was going to be a chilly night, but I didn't notice myself shivering until the sun started to go down and I was already most of the way home. I considered not turning back for it, but I figured that since I had the keys anyway, I might as well run back into the library, scoop it up, and be out of there.

As soon as I entered the building I knew something was wrong. I heard what sounded like a rhythmic hum, like there was some kind of generator running. But all the lights were off. I decided to ignore it and just look for my jacket, but the deeper I got into the library, the louder it got. At that point I was too curious to let it go, so I started to follow the noise. It led me to the stairs, and I realized it was coming from the second floor. From the Reading Room. In that moment I knew that whatever was happening, Damion was behind it.

I crept up the marble stairs. As I walked down the second floor hall, I realized the hum was actually a chant. The same chant that Damion made the kids do. But this time, they weren't saying it like a nursery rhyme. They were repeating it like...a plea.

I gently pushed the door to the Reading Room open, knowing that Damion would not be pleased to find me snooping. I feared what he might do to me if he found I was there. All the kids were seated on their cushions, hands pressed over their eyes, repeating that horrible chant. The only light in the room was the moonlight streaming in through the huge windows, casting long shadows of the children across the floor. Damion sat in the rocking chair, his face almost glowing in the moonlight, grinning.

"Now," he whispered, "it's time to crown the Summer Reading Champion."

With a flourish, he lifted one of the "reading logs " and a little girl stood up. I recognized her from Read Aloud as Lucy, a shy three-year-old. I had spent a lot of my volunteer time sitting her in my lap and encouraging her to interact with the other kids.

"Thank you for choosing me," she said in a voice that was not hers. "I am honored."

Slowly she glided through the other children and towards Damion, who stood with an outstretched hand at the front of the room.

I'm not sure what I thought was going to happen. Even looking back, I still have no idea what might have happened if that girl had taken Damion's hand. But I had this sense of dread deep in my stomach, this knowledge that if he touched that little girl, something irreversible would happen, and it would be terrible and it would be all my fault for doing nothing.

Without thinking about it, I leapt forward, dashing through the children and scooping up Lucy in my arms. Damion cried out in surprise when I appeared. I guess he hadn't seen me lurking in the shadows in the back of the room.

"The child now belongs to me," he said in a voice I know did not come from him.

"No," I told him, "she doesn't. And you are ruining the Summer Reading Program."

I shifted Lucy to my left arm to free up my right, and I smacked him across the face. I didn't actually hit that hard, but I think it was the surprise of it that made him give an inhuman shriek, reeling backwards. The moment he fell, it was as though a spell was broken. The children simply stood up and left. Even Lucy wriggled out of my arms and walked towards the door. When I looked down, Damion was gone, and I was alone in the Reading Room.

I know I sound crazy, especially since none of the kids remember this happening, but you can ask Laura. She'll back me up. Damion was there, and he did...he did *something* to those poor kids, even if they don't remember it. And then he just...disappeared.

You may think that after all this, I would never want to set foot in the library again, and that was true. For like a week. But I missed the kids, and I missed Read Aloud, so I picked up where Randy left off and started reading those kids books myself. I don't think I want to go to college anymore since it seems like I've got a pretty sweet gig lined up right here, so it turns out all that "community engagement" was for nothing. Well, not for nothing. I'm pretty happy. Mostly.

I still often wonder what happened to Randy. And I never stay in the library after dark.

Steve Goes Home

I don't have much time, so I'll be brief: Gonzalez is dead, and I'm getting out of here while I still have the chance. Yes, I know you're probably on your way to get me, but you're sure taking your sweet time, aren't ya? I mean, I imagine you said to yourself, "hey, our Mars research station has stopped sending us data on neat rocks, and we can't seem to reach them." And then once you made that revelation you would have figured something had gone awry and hauled your asses up here. But I know it's a long trip to get up here, even though I know you must be close by now, I think I'm out of time. I've been waiting, and you haven't shown, so I'm taking off on my own terms.

It was one of our O2 tanks that blew. Gonzalez was caught in the blast. I don't wanna talk about it more than that. If you really need more details, I left tons of voice logs on the console. It was...I didn't take it well. Honestly all that disaster training we did before coming up here really went out the window once she was gone. I went a little berserk. I mean, not only did most of our food supply and our experimental equipment burn; I also lost my only companion up here. Gonzalez and I — well, we had our differences. She didn't like the way I did things, I didn't like the way she was such a hardass. But at the end of the day we were colleagues, and I think by the time of the— by the time she passed away, I think we were something like friends.

You don't realize how difficult it is to dig Mars dust until you're making a grave for your research partner. For every scoop of sandy red soil I tossed over my shoulder, a little cascade of dust poured right back into my hole. It took me a whole Martian day, but I finally buried her. I buried her in her space suit. It's not like she needed it any more. It just felt wrong to give her body to the dirt, unprotected. She needed a casket of sorts, and what better than the kevlar she swore by? Besides, she was...there wasn't much left of her. It was a pretty funeral that way, her...remains tucked safely away in that suit, so I could maintain the illusion that she still looked human. With her, I buried all my hopes of survival. Almost no food, most of our equipment gone. I had enough to continue our research, but I wouldn't have much luck studying mineral samples if I'd already starved to death. So I sat at her sandy grave until the sun went down, then trudged back to the station to live out the meager days I had left.

That's when the knocking started.

I knew from the briefing that we had been the only human mission on Mars. That left only two options: space weather, or extraterrestrial life decided to very politely announce itself by knocking on my door. But neither checked out: all the sensors confirmed that weather conditions were ideal, and you know as well as I do that Mars can't support life. So what the hell was banging on the airlock? Each time I heard the knocking and ran to the surveillance system to check it out, the visitor was gone.

I know what you're thinking: the best idea would have been for me to leave the whole thing alone. I went through basic training just like you, but even if I didn't, like, I've seen *Alien*. I know you don't mess with the scary monster or there will be chest-bursting consequences. But like I said, I wasn't thinking straight. I was probably more...reckless than I should have been. When I finally caught the thing on camera, I couldn't help but investigate.

I'm not sure what I thought I'd see. A bug-eyed green man in a flying saucer? But what I saw was — well, I'm not sure we really have words for it, but the thought that sprung to mind was, "whoa, that's a giant robot." Not one of *our* robots. I'm not saying Perseverance or Fortitude came to crash at our research station. I'm saying what looked like a *massive mech* was banging on the outer airlock hatch with a huge metal fist. Honestly I was relieved. I was not scientifically, psychologically, or emotionally prepared to make first contact. But a robot? That I could deal with. I hadn't put together how the hell it had gotten up here, but I assumed I could figure all that out once I let R2-D2 in. Besides, I was almost out of food anyway. I'd rather die in a sick space battle than starve.

I know Gonzalez would have hated me for it, but I did the only thing I could think to do: I opened the airlock. And the machine clomped in.

The "robot" was vaguely humanoid in that it walked on two mechanical legs, but instead of a torso there was only a glimmering black pod, like an egg so large it could fit a whole person. A mechanical arm extended from the top of the pod, topped with a spindly metal claw. I looked up at the shimmering black sphere as if it were a giant eye, but in it I only saw my own reflection, stretched and distorted.

Then with a hiss, the pod split in two down the center. With a mechanical whir the crack widened, revealing what was inside. And that's when I felt my stomach twist and my limbs tremble because in that moment I realized this was *not* a robot. It was just a container, a container for a *creature,* and that creature wanted to meet me face to face.

The being that emerged from the egg looked a bit like a bear, with scruffy brown fur and long claws, but it's face was about half the size of its body, round and flat with a wet crack running across the middle that I can only assume was a mouth, full of sparkling metallic stumps that I imagine were some version of teeth. Above the slimy opening was a little black orb about the size of a Magic 8-Ball that kept flicking around, so I assumed that was an eye, taking the place in. Extending from above the eye were what I can only describe as fuzzy tentacles. It stepped two hulking furry legs out of the suit, but they weren't legs, they were...they were tendrils, and the weight of its body was so extreme that the whole station shook when it placed its feet. Okay, now that I say it out loud, I guess it didn't really look anything like a bear. But it was big and furry is what I'm trying to say.

The eye darted around the room before it settled on me.

The mouth began to leak some kind of bile, and I realized that this was probably it for me — I was the first human to make contact with extraterrestrial life, and I was going to be eaten by a giant space bear.

"Um," I stammered, staring up into the black orb, dwarfed by the towering creature, "Please don't eat me."

I'm not sure why I said anything; obviously this creature couldn't speak English. But it *responded*.

The creature produced a sort of gurgling sound from somewhere in its bowels, and it clacked its shiny teeth together in a rhythmic pattern. A furry tentacle reached for me, and I braced myself for it to wrap around me and drop me in the creature's gaping mouth. I squeezed my eyes shut and hoped that it would be painless.

It patted me on the head.

I opened an eye and saw that the creature was — well, I can't really be sure about this, but I think it was *smiling*. And when it gurgled, I could have sworn it sounded *happy*. Maybe it was all in my head. But suddenly the creature was satisfied, like it had done what it came here to do, and after rustling my hair a bit it bounded back into its mechanized space suit, and the metallic casing closed around it. It bounded off to the airlock and banged to indicate that our meeting was over.

Numb with shock and fear, I made my way over to the console and did as the creature requested. And then it was gone.

Now, I wish I could say that I handled all of this like the calm and collected scientist that you know me to be. But I definitely didn't. The moment I was alone again, I collapsed, bawling. The psychological weight of having been the first human to make first contact was mixing with the terror of thinking I was about to be devoured alive by a huge space creature, and all of that was a little much for me. And then there was the knowledge that Gonzalez would have killed for the opportunity to see that Martian with me, and she was long gone.

Wait.

No.

Not a Martian.

Because a Martian wouldn't need a spacesuit.

"You don't belong here either," I said aloud as I watched the creature disappear from our visual sensors. "You're an alien just like me."

I named him Steve.

In retrospect I probably should have used a cool "science" name, like Galileo or Kelvin or Beaker or whatever. But I don't know, he just felt like a Steve? He also felt like a he. Not sure why. Don't think aliens have gender.

When Steve came back the next time, I wasn't scared. Well, that's not true. I was still terrified because, let's be real, from my perspective he was a hulking monster that could crush my bones like uncooked spaghetti, so yeah, of course I was scared of him. But if he wanted to hurt me, I think he would have done it already. So this time I let him in without hesitation.

He did the same routine as before — clomping in with his mech, then unpeeling himself when he was safely inside. Guess he breathed oxygen too.

"Hey Steve," I greeted him, having promised myself that this time I would at least *pretend* not to be terrified. "What's shakin', bacon?"

He responded with a short gurgle and two clacks, then he extended a furry paw and pulled a metal box from the claw at the end of his space suit's arm. He placed it on the ground between us. And he waited.

"Do you...do you want me to take that? Is that for me?" I asked, pointing at the box. He wiggled his furry tentacles.

"Is that a yes?"

Wiggle.

"Okay...just...just don't eat me if I do something wrong, okay?"

Tentatively, I knelt down and opened the box. With a yelp, I recoiled when I saw a red liquid sloshing around inside.

"Oh god!" I screamed, "What the — what is that? Is that —" I cut myself off before I asked him if he had brought me a box full of blood.

As if in answer, Steve lowered one of his furry tentacles into the red liquid, and once it was coated in the stuff, he lifted it to his wet crack of a mouth and slurped it off.

"This is...this is *food?*" I asked.

Gurgle.

Oh, what the hell, I thought, *what do I have to lose?* I leaned over and I lapped some of it up.

And get this: It was delicious.

It's hard to describe since we don't really have anything like it on Earth, but I'd say it was like if whipped cream and vinegar had a baby, but that baby was somehow a thick stew. Well that makes it sound bad — but I swear, it was the best thing I'd ever tasted. As I sat back up and wiped the space-soup away with the back of my hand, the creature gave what must have been a gurgle of contentment. Then it gave another quick gurgle and two clacks like it had when it first entered.

"Urgh-clack-clack?" I attempted to repeat. He wiggled his tentacles in approval, then leapt back into his suit, and he was off as quickly as he'd come.

This time, I practiced mimicking his sounds so that when he inevitably returned bearing another box of soup, I could take a swing at communication.

"Urgh-clack-clack," I repeated. "Is that...is that...is that my name?" I pointed to myself.

Wiggles. I was beginning to understand that the wiggles were akin to a head-nod.

"I'm Urgh-Clack-Clack," I declared, "and you," I pointed, "are Steve."

The creature hissed, and at first I thought I had angered it. Then I realized it was struggling to make sounds.

"Sssss" it hissed, "ssssss-CLACK. Sssssss-CLACK-aaaaaa."

"What are you —"

"Sss-CLACK-eeee."

"Steve?"

"Sss-CLACK-eeeefffff."

"Steve, you did it!" I leapt up, clapping my hands, "You said your name! I'm Urgh-Clack-Clack —"

Wiggles.

"And you're Steve!"

Satisfied gurgles.

We shared some space soup that night, his tentacle resting over my shoulder like a protective hand.

It must have been a few months since Steve's first visit when I started collecting samples again. If I'm honest, I started to lose track of time with Gonzalez gone. Now it's not that I'm not perfectly capable of looking at a watch, just that...well, when I was all alone everything seemed hopeless; these things just seemed to slip away from me. Once Steve and I were buddies, though, I started keeping track of time again. I even started making up my own day of the week.

It was Bloosday when I finally decided to get back to the neat rocks. I figured, hey, enough moping: you've got a friend now, Urgh-clack-clack! Time to do what you were sent here to do. The folks down on Earth are going to come for you, and they'll be expecting some cool data on rocks. So get back to it!

Admittedly, it was nice to have a task to throw myself into again. Now that I wasn't worried about starving to death — I had plenty of Steve's space soup — I could spend time doing something that wasn't ruminating on my imminent demise. So I threw on my suit and started collecting samples.

I had been out there for a few hours when I heard the familiar mechanical creaking of another spacesuit.

"Steve!" I called out, though I knew he couldn't hear. I saw him bounding over the rocks to come greet me, shifting his head back and forth rhythmically, which was what he always did when something confused him. It was the Steve-equivalent of raising one's voice at the end of a question. And the implicit question was, "What are you doing out here?" He placed a tentacle to his mouth to indicate eating. This was how he usually asked me if I was hungry.

"No, Steve," I shook my head. "I'm not looking for food."

I lifted one of my rock samples and gestured toward the station, to communicate that I was only gathering the rocks to bring them back. I wasn't sure how to communicate a concept as complicated as collecting geological data and relaying it back to Earth, so I settled for expressing the simple idea of a collection.

From inside the suit I could hear the sound of "playful burbles," like the sounds a cat makes when you wave a ribbon in front of it. He bounded around the rust-orange rocks, collecting them in a pile for me. While I couldn't see his furry face through the visor of his suit, I could just tell from his jittery bouncing that he was excited. And I could tell that he was watching me, waiting for my approval.

"Yes" and "no" were well-worn concepts for us at this point. Steve would often try to mess around with my equipment in the station, and he got the message pretty quickly that I didn't like that. So when I nodded my head that yes, I *did* like it when Steve collected samples for me, he leapt off to go gather more stones.

By the end of the day I had far more rocks than I needed, and likely they would just end up cluttering the inside of the station. Nevertheless, Steve continued to bring me rocks even in the days after, along with the big box of space soup. He'd seen a wide range of my emotions at this point, so I'm pretty sure he could tell that I was delighted — not just to have new samples, but at the fact that he was bringing me *gifts*. I wished I could give him something in return, but he seemed perfectly content to give me a pat on the head and share some space soup.

And I suppose this is where I address the current situation. You see, I kinda loved living with Steve like this, but I knew it couldn't go on forever.

One day Steve came over and he had a sense of...urgency. He was gurgling like crazy, leaking saliva all over the console, teeth clacking away, tentacles wriggling.

"What's going on, buddy?" I asked. "Is something wrong?"

He pulled my space suit from the cabinet and dragged it out in front of me.

"You want me to go out?" I asked as I began to suit up.

Anxious wiggles.

Once we were out in the red desert, he led me over the crest of the hill that overlooked the research station. And when I saw what lay just beyond I gave a sharp gasp.

I'd been over this hill thousands of times. I knew there wasn't anything *here*. Which is why I was pretty shocked to discover that planted in the middle of the red sands was a thin metallic pyramid, reaching into the clouds like a giant hand stretched it into the sky, pulling it to an impossible height. It must have been ten times the size of the research station. No, more. It was like looking up at a skyscraper, but a skyscraper where you know there should definitely *not* be a skyscraper, like if the Empire State Building had appeared in the middle of Kansas.

Do you know that feeling when you're standing right next to the train tracks when the train rushes by you, and for a brief moment you are reminded of how small you are compared to the mechanical beast that just passed? Or when you're standing at the foot of a famous monument and you realize for the first time how *huge* the thing really is, so huge you can feel it in your stomach? But for some reason instead of making you feel scared or insignificant, it does the opposite: it makes you feel happy. There's this inexplicable rush of serotonin when you experience something — well, something big.

I felt like that. But more.

I knew I was seeing the thing with my own eyes, and yet I still felt like I was seeing something bigger than I could possibly comprehend.

And somehow I just knew that this was a spaceship.

Steve's people had come for him.

"Are you...are you saying goodbye?" I asked. And believe it or not, I felt my throat tighten, and tears welled up in my eyes. "Don't go, Steve," I murmured.

He wrapped his mech-hand gingerly around my arm and pulled me towards the ship.

That's when I understood.

"You want me to *come*?" I pointed to myself, then the ship.

I heard affirmative gurgles, and I can only assume inside the suit there was some joyous wriggling. I glanced back from the ship to the station we'd trekked from at the base of the red hill. I'd spent — well, honestly I have no idea at this point how long I've been there. Must have been half a year since Gonzalez died. Maybe more. And before the fire, we'd already been together up there for a year and a half. I'd developed a bit of an affection for the place, I guess. But the place wasn't going to keep me alive. The place wasn't going to care for me.

I knew that in this moment, the relationship we had spent months building was on the precipice of crashing down. Because through all that time together, for all our invented sounds and signals and painstakingly crafted forms of communication, we had never once communicated the concept of time. How could I ever express to Steve that I needed him to *wait*?

Maybe I should have said "to hell with it," took his mechanical hand, and bounded towards the ship. But I still had Gonzalez's voice bouncing around in my head, chastising me for not following proper protocol. In all the time I'd been with Steve, I'd never left one log. I'd made first contact and if I left now, no one would ever know that it happened. Then again, if I went back to the station and Steve thought this was my farewell, I'd be doomed to starve in the station alone, without my only friend.

"Steve," I looked up at him pleadingly, knowing my words meant nothing to him, "I want to go with you. I do. But I need to go back to the station first. I need..." I kept instinctively gesturing to my wrist to indicate a watch, even though these signals would be lost on him. "I need time."

He made a soft, mournful gurgle, and the sound was so pitiful I could feel tears burning my eyes. I extended my arm to him, gesturing for him to come closer. At least this he could understand. The mechanical legs of his suit groaned as he leaned the black orb that held his body towards me. I placed my gloved hands around the sphere and gently laid my head on the metal of his suit. Our visors met with a near imperceptible *clink*. I knew that no words, no gestures, could possibly express what I needed to tell him: *I'm not leaving you*.

After that, I ran back to the station, sending silent prayers to whatever god would listen that I would not miss my chance to flee with Steve.

And here I am. You know what's weird? I trust him. For all our stories of alien abduction and human experimentation, I'm not afraid of any of that. Maybe they *are* going to experiment on me. I don't really mind. But Steve and I? We're buddies. I don't think he'll let them hurt me.

So if you're listening to this log, one of two things must have happened: Steve left without me, and without any source of food or any kind of companionship, I wasted away up here. You came too late. But I'm assuming if that's the case you've already sorted that out, because you've probably found my body. So if I'm not anywhere to be found, well, that leaves the second option: Steve waited for me.

Gonzalez, if you're somehow listening up there, well, I hope you're happy. I'm gonna head back out there now, and if all goes well, then Steve will take me home.

What I Wouldn't Do for Annie

Michael always ordered a strawberry banana smoothie with protein powder.

"Bleh," you would say, "I hate bananas. Protein powder I can handle, but banana?"

I'd smile at your voice, and I'd slide the plastic cup across the counter, usually announcing it with something vulgar, like "Here's you drink, dickhead," instead of what I'm supposed to say: "Keep it loosy goosy with Mister Juicy."

That always made him smile. I only did it because he left me a bigger tip. All it took was a lewd comment to make him grin, and he'd drop some coins in the tin and say, "Here's something for your *tit* jar," and I'd pretend that it was funny.

"I wouldn't exactly call this place cozy," you often said, sitting at your usual table right by the register, eyeing the bright pink tiling on the walls and the lime green counter, shifting around in your metal chair. But it didn't need to be cozy — Mister Juicy was *our* place. It's not like anyone else from our school was hanging out at a tacky juice bar every afternoon. Most days we'd joke, make big plans we both knew we'd never follow through on, and steal the occasional carton of berries when my manager wasn't looking. But then Michael would show up, and you and I would share a knowing gaze, and you would start doing your homework and I would start chopping bananas.

"That for Mr. Thompson?" I nodded to the blank document on your laptop.

"Yeah. Old creep."

I shook my head. "Can't stand that guy," I mumbled.

And then, of course, Michael came in. He nodded to you as usual and you rolled your eyes, but even I wasn't sure whether or not you were secretly pleased at the acknowledgement.

"Cas? You know what to do."

"Yeah, yeah, I know," I said, already grabbing some strawberries and giving them a rinse.

"You ever read Nietzche, Cas?" he asked, leaning against the bar.

I shrugged. "We have AP euro together, remember? I learned about the same crusty old guys as you. Or did you forget I'm in that class?"

He carried on, ignoring my jibe. "Well, I've been reading *Thus Spoke Zarathustra* and I gotta say —"

"Cas!" you interrupted, "Kiwi me!"

I tossed you a kiwi slice and you caught it daintily in your mouth. He was watching. It made my stomach twist. I don't know why.

He turned back to me.

"Why don't you ever kiwi *me*, Cas?"

I pelted him with a kiwi slice right between the eyes. For one fraction of a second his face went hard. I felt fear shoot through my stomach. Fear of *what* I'm not sure, but for a moment I panicked that I'd made a horrible mistake, that I'd enraged him, that he was about to sweep his arm across the counter and smash all the glasses I'd just cleaned. Then he laughed. I laughed. It wasn't funny.

I slid him the smoothie.

"There you go, asshole."

He smiled. Then his attention was on you, and suddenly I felt like I was no one.

"So Annie," he sauntered over to your table and dropped into a chair, "I like that shirt."

I didn't need to be watching to know that his eyes darted to your chest.

"Thanks," you said with your usual uncertainty, toying with that necklace I gave you for your birthday two years ago. "I need to get back to my essay."

You tilted your head to the left so the two of us could share a glance and I almost started laughing, because I know for a fact that you won't start that essay until the moment it's due.

"The *Catcher In The Rye* one?" he asked. "Don't worry about that, I'll tell you everything you need to know."

"I could do that too," I interrupted. "Whiny bitch boy can't get laid, wears a dorky hat. There. Essay done."

Genuine anger flashed across his face, same as the moment the kiwi hit him. "It's a lot more complicated than —"

"No, actually, I already wrote that down," you responded, closing your laptop as you ran a hand through your hair. "Essay done."

He began explaining the "nuances" and "culture references" in the "historical masterpiece" while I mimed whacking him with an imaginary baseball bat behind the counter. You stifled a giggle.

"What?" he asked.

"No, no, keep going. I'm learning so much," your face was turning bright red. He picked back up and I mimed slicing his head off with my knife.

This got a hearty laugh from you.

"What?" he demanded again. "What's so funny?" He whirled back around to look at me, but I was already back to chopping fruit. He stood so abruptly that his chair shot back against the counter with a bang, making me jump.

"Forget about it," he grumbled, adding something under his breath about having homework to do anyway, stomping towards the door and leaving his partially-drunk smoothie behind.

"Ugh," you said, lifting the container by the cap as if it were dead fish. "Banana." You tossed it towards the trash and missed dramatically, spattering the wall with pink.

It was the last "normal" day I ever knew.

§

"Hear about Brooke?" Michael asked as he plopped himself down in the metal chair on the other side of your table. I felt a pang shoot through my stomach.

"Yeah," you said without looking up from what you were doing, which I'm fairly certain was watching anime. "It sucks. Jason should have known better than to take those pictures at the party. And it was dick move to post them."

"Oh I don't know about that," he leaned back in his chair, sucking on his straw, "I mean, don't you think this is what she wanted. I mean, c'mon," Michael goaded. I couldn't see his face but I knew he was wearing that victorious smirk, the one he put on when he finally got a rise out of you. "Obviously she just did it for the attention."

"Obviously she was *drunk*," you corrected.

"Yeah but you know what they say: when you're drunk you become your truest self. And she definitely showed her true self alright."

"You can't just —" you struggled to choose your words, your face beginning to redden with frustration. "You can't just say shit like that!"

"Jesus, you're so sensitive!" he rolled his eyes. "I can say whatever I want. Or have you not heard of free speech?" He took a long sip of his smoothie and mumbled, "So much for the tolerant left, amirite?"

Please stop talking, I begged internally. *Please stop. Please stop.* He sipped his smoothie in silence and I breathed a sigh of relief. I felt wetness on my fingers and I discovered I'd been squeezing a kiwi so hard that my fingernails had dug into the flesh and the juice was dripping down my wrist. I tossed it in the trash. You went back to the anime you were watching on your laptop instead of doing homework. I sucked in a deep breath and picked up my fruit knife.

"And she's hot, too," he continued.

"You looked at the pictures?" your head snapped back up.

"It's what she wants!" Michael defended, gesturing with his smoothie hand.

"No it's not!"

"Sure that's what she says, but, c'mon —"

"Despite what you may think, Michael," you leaned in, hand punctuating each of your words, "girls aren't always doing things for attention."

"Well what about you?" he countered. I could feel my whole body tense. "I mean, look at the clothes you wear."

"What...*about* the clothes I wear?" you seethed, choosing her words deliberately.

"I mean, you're not fooling anyone. You dress so men will find you hot. You wear those shirts to show off your little boobs and you wear those heels to show off your ass — it's not like it's a secret who you're doing it for."

"I'm not doing it for *men*!" you snapped, standing up so abruptly that your chair screeched on the tiles.

Michael laughed. "Well it's not like you're doing it for yourself."

"What makes you so —"

"You don't even like to look at yourself!"

A moment of icy silence.

"What are you talking about?" you demanded.

"Cameron told me about how you quit drama class because you didn't like changing in front of a mirror with other girls. Everyone said it was because you were gay and because being around a ton of naked girls made you too horny or something, but Cameron said it was because of the mirror. Like you didn't like to see yourself naked. So I know you're not doing it because you wanna look at yourself. So who does that leave?"

"Who..." you searched for words, your eyes flicking around wildly like a caged animal looking for escape. The next thing out of your mouth was the last thing I expected.

"Who's been saying I'm gay?"

Michael scoffed. "Who isn't? Everyone thinks that you and Cas are like, a thing," he nodded his head in my direction.

For a moment I feared you would laugh. I knew you wouldn't, but for a second I could imagine you glancing at me, nose wrinkled in disgust, shouting, "Yeah, like I would date *that*!"

But that's not what you did. You took a moment to think and then you said, "Cas is not a girl."

Michael stood up and glanced in my direction, eyes running over me appraisingly.

"Cas is basically a girl," he concluded.

"No, they're not," you said. He shrugged.

"Look, you can use whatever labels you want," he put his hands up as though he were under attack, "but the way I see it, if it has tits, it's a girl."

"Oh, so Cas is an 'it' to you?" you neared the counter, gesturing to me, and I wanted to slink back and hide.

"No," Michael responded levelly, as though he were talking to a child, "Cas is a 'she' to me, but apparently if I say that, I get canceled."

This time you laughed. A humorless chuckle dripping with rage.

"Canceled?" you repeated. "No, you don't get 'canceled.' You just...you just become a dick!"

"I'd rather be a dick than a sensitive little —"

"Shut up!" you screamed.

"Awww, did I make you mad?" he mocked, giving an exaggerated pout.

Suddenly both of you were staring at me. It took me a moment to realize that I had snorted.

"What's so funny, Cas?" Michael asked, and beneath the calm of his voice I could hear that there was something else underneath, something dangerous.

Don't say it, I told myself. *Stay quiet. That's what you always do with him. You don't say it, and you stay quiet.* But the counter between us, it somehow felt like protection, like a little lime-green shield, and I just couldn't stop myself from —

"I just think it's funny," I said, "That you're calling her the sensitive one, but you flipped your shit when I called Holden Caulfield an incel."

"I didn't flip my —"

"You did, though," you backed me up, crossing your arms, "You were all, 'You stupid hoes don't understand the nuance of —"

"Well you *didn't* understand the nuance —"

"Of course I understand the nuance," I cut him off before I could stop myself. "I'm smart, Michael. And just because I don't care about half the shit you talk about doesn't mean I'm a total idiot. But you take it all so goddamn seriously! Don't you have a sense of humor?"

"Of course I have a —"

I threw a kiwi at him.

You laughed. You laughed so hard I thought you were crying. You laughed so hard I thought you were losing your mind. Maybe you were.

"Stop it!" he yelled at you. "Stop laughing!" Whatever rage I had seen simmering behind his eyes every once in a while, it was beginning to boil now. That familiar fear I often felt churning in my stomach returned, but this time it wasn't a fleeting sensation. I rushed around the bar, not bothering to put down the fruit knife.

"Dude! Calm down!" I said.

"Make her stop laughing! Make her stop!" His face was going red, the veins in his neck bulging, his hands clenched into fists.

In that moment I was absolutely certain he was going to hurt someone. I don't know how I knew. All I can say is that there was violence in his eyes. I could read it as clearly as though it was written. Like this was some warped version of *Catcher in the Rye* where Holden craves blood. I don't know if it was me he wanted to hurt or if it was you or if it was every woman he'd ever met, but he was going to hurt someone and I knew this without a doubt.

"You need to chill," I commanded, holding up my hands defensively but afraid to get any closer, fruit knife dripping strawberry juice down my forearm.

What do I do if he hits her? I asked myself. *What do I do if he hits me? What do I do?*

But he never touched you.

"Shut up or I will make you," he threatened.

You stopped laughing. "What did you just say?" you asked.

He took one step closer to you. He didn't need to speak, and he didn't need to touch you— his towering form over your small frame said more than he ever could with words. *I am bigger than you. I could hurt you. If I wanted.*

You grabbed the fruit knife out of my hand before I had time to react and you slashed. You didn't threaten, you didn't give a warning, you didn't even make a sound. You just slashed.

You slashed his throat.

I'd never seen someone choke on their own blood before until that moment.

His eyes went wide as he grasped at his neck, unable to stop the blood that poured forth. He gasped for air that wouldn't reach his lungs as he stumbled then fell to his knees. He looked up at you, eyes scared and almost pleading, then flopped forward, spewing crimson on both of our legs. He looked like a fish flopping around on a dock, wheezing, gurgling, whining.

And then he stopped.

For a moment we just stayed there in a grotesque tableau, three of us motionless, one of us lifeless. You and I simply stood there, watching the blood spread across the floor and seep into the soles of our shoes. For a fleeting moment, there was complete stillness.

And then I said, "My manager is gonna be pissed!"

You took a deep breath. You looked at me. And then you ran, taking the bloody knife with you.

§

"So you'd say this kid Michael...he was bullying your friend Annie, yes?" one of the police officers asked. The question made me want to throw up. Bullying? It wasn't bullying. It was...I don't know what it was, but bullying was such a juvenile way to put it. But I didn't have the right words. So I just nodded. The police officer shook his head.

"That's the way it always goes. Kids get bullied, and then just..." he snapped his fingers. "Good thing no one gave this girl a gun, or maybe she would have shot up the place."

At that point I did actually throw up. Kale smoothie everywhere.

§

"I heard she ripped out his heart and started eating it like an animal. Is that true?"

"I heard he was pleading for his life and she killed him anyway."

"Someone told me he just walked in and she shot him in the face."

I should have cleared your name. I should have told them that you were defending yourself, defending me, and that you weren't a killer. Instead I said I was in the backroom getting more fruit. That by the time I ran out to see what was happening you were already gone, and blood was already pooling on the hot pink tile floor. That I hadn't seen anything. That I didn't know anything.

Oh god, Annie. You could have eaten his heart. I can imagine it.

They put me in counseling, naturally. They pulled me out of my art class so that I could sit in a scratchy maroon chair across from a woman with long gray hair and a glasses chain who was completely underqualified for this position.

"You must still be hurting from the death of your friend," she would say.

No. It wasn't my friend who died. It was my friend who disappeared.

But I couldn't say that. I couldn't say, "*Actually I think the murderer was correct and I support her. I think the world is a better place without Michael. I think he was going to really hurt people someday. To hurt women. To hurt anything and anyone he didn't understand.*"

"It is hard," I said, eyes brimming with tears, tears my counselor thought I shed over Michael, tears that I knew were about something else entirely. "It is so, so hard."

§

They didn't make me go to the memorial service. I'm at least thankful for that. But when the student council organized a 5k in his honor, the posters were everywhere. His name was everywhere. In the hallways, on a banner in the cafeteria, on the school website, on the morning announcements. Did anyone ever think about me? Did they ever once think about what it would do to me?

"I hope they find that girl," my math teacher said. Maybe she forgot that I was in the class. Maybe she said it because she *knew* that I was in the class. "Bring that bitch to justice. That's what I say. Going around killing poor babies...it ain't right."

Yeah. Like I could have focused on doing conic sections after that.

My parents asked me what they could do to help. They said I'd been so quiet, they were afraid that I'd stop speaking altogether. I told them I didn't need anything.

Which wasn't true, but it's not as though they could give me anything I needed. I needed my best friend.

I quit the job at Mister Juicy, as you might have been able to guess. Or maybe I got fired, actually. I'm not really sure. Either way I was definitely not walking into that hot-pink-tiled hell ever again. I just knew that it would smell like blood. Yes, I knew they cleaned it. It would still smell like blood.

So I started walking home straight from school, something I never used to do. And the whole time I would try not to remember the days that you and me would walk home together, laughing about the stupid thing old Mr. Thompson had said in class, or about the dudes in the truck who had just catcalled you, or more often some inside joke of our own devising. In fact, I often tried not to think at all during my walks home, which is why I was so startled when I felt a hand descend over my mouth and yank me to my left. Before I had the presence of mind to resist I was stumbling into an alley and shoved up against a wall.

And there you were.

"Don't make any noise," you whispered, and then you let me go. "I don't have much time, so we have to make this quick."

For the first moment, I just looked at you. It had been years since I'd seen you without makeup, and I almost didn't recognize your face when the only thing it was painted with was dirt. You wore the same outfit that you had that day, but it was stained and ripped. Your long hair, usually so neatly brushed and parted, was wild and caked with mud. But you were still wearing that necklace I had given you, and even in your urgency you were fiddling with it.

I think it was the most beautiful I'd ever seen you. I just stared.

Truth be told, I thought you'd left. I imagined you cruising in a stolen car, leaning out the window, your hair streaming in the wind, off to find a new life with a new name in, oh, I don't know...Santa Fe? Not sure why I thought Santa Fe, but I could just see you living your new life in the desert. Away from everything.

"What — what are you still doing here?" I stammered. "You need to go! You need to leave! They'll — if they find you —" I'm not sure who "they" was. Anyone, really.

"Cas, listen to me," you hissed. "I can't leave."

"What — what do you mean you can't leave?"

"Do you know how it felt, Cas?"

I didn't need to ask what you meant. How it felt to kill. How it felt to take the life of the man — boy? Man — who had plagued you for so long, who fed the beast inside you, but the wrong beast, the beast that was trying to devour you from the inside out, who was slowly killing you, killing us both, with every comment and backhanded compliment and put-down. How it felt to make him bleed.

"It was amazing," you whispered, and I could hear the thirst in your voice. "It was...it was like a drug."

"Annie…" I murmured, my whole body quivering, "you're scaring me."

Your eyes darkened. I don't know how it's possible, but they did. "I need to do it again, Cas."

"What? You want to — you want to kill someone else?"

"Someone who deserves it. No one else will do it. So it's up to me."

"Wha — No! Annie, do you hear yourself? You sound — I mean, I can't keep defending this. I can't keep defending *you*!" Which was a lie. I hadn't been defending you, not out loud.

"I never asked you to defend me," you shot back, then sucked in a deep breath. "But I am asking you to come with me."

I stared at you, wordless.

"You want me…to murder someone…with you?" I finally managed to put the words together. You nodded.

And you know what? I actually wanted to do it. Not because I shared the same bloodlust that had been awakened in you. Because I looked at you and I still knew that despite everything, I wanted to do anything for you. I wanted to do what you asked me because I wanted to see you smile, a genuine smile, because I loved you.

"Annie…I can't," I remember my voice catching in my throat and I'm pretty sure tears began to cloud my vision. "I just can't. It would mean giving up everything and…I can't give up my life for you. I'm sorry."

Your face fell.

"Of course you don't want to give up your life. You've always been happier than me," you said. I wanted to protest, but I bit it down. I certainly never felt happier than you. I think I was always a bit jealous of you, honestly. You were always the beautiful one. But when it comes to happiness, beauty is a useless currency. I knew something darker lurked behind your rouged cheeks and painted lips, something that no matter how close our friendship grew, you wouldn't be able to talk about. You didn't have the words. I didn't either.

So I swallowed the envy I carried with me for years and I nodded. I was happier than you. That was easy enough to accept.

"I couldn't keep living like that," you continued. "Something needed to change or I —" you cut yourself off, turning away from me. "Take care of yourself, Cas."

§

I saw it on Facebook first.

"I can't believe you're gone, bro. I'll miss you."

"One of the best young men and promising young athletes I've ever known. Heaven gained another angel today."

"You were a great friend and a great person. You will be missed."

Jason Cunningham. The one who took those pictures of Brooke and posted them. He disappeared after baseball practice and was found dead in the woods. But it got worse. His heart was carved out, just like in those rumors about Michael. It was found a few yards away, discarded in the dirt. It looked like someone had taken a bite out of it.

And you know what I thought? It's horrible, I know, but I saw the news and I laughed. Because in my head I heard Michael, sipping on his strawberry banana smoothie and mumbling, "So much for the tolerant left, amirite?"

§

"Maneater." I hope you were able to hear about that. That's what they started calling you. You know, like when serial killers get a nickname? You weren't a serial killer, of course. You only had two kills under your belt. But you were well on your way and everyone was antsy about when the Maneater would strike again.

Sports practices were canceled.

"No need to endanger our boys before all this is sorted out," the football coach said at one assembly. It's not like you were gonna be going after the star quarterback. But that's the funny thing — they were *so* scared of you anyway. Because they used to be safe — *boys* used to be safe — and now the Maneater could come for anyone.

Still, the last thing anyone expected was that you would go for an old man.

Old Mr. Thompson, notorious groper, harasser, and all around creep, didn't show up to school on Tuesday. The body was on the football field. The heart was in the gym.

My best friend. A serial killer. I'm kinda proud, honestly. How many lives would Jason have ruined? How many more students would Mr. Thompson have traumatized? How many lives did you save? I don't know the answer. Maybe none. Maybe hundreds.

My best friend. The Maneater. It was like a superhero name. Goddamn, Annie. Goddamn.

§

"Hey," my mom said in a voice that was too gentle to mean anything good. "We wanted to be the ones to tell you before you saw it online."

I told you they'd find you. I told you to leave. But you didn't listen.

"Police shootout" they called it. Yeah right. You didn't have a gun. And even if you did I know for a fact you wouldn't have had a clue how to fire it. You posed no threat to police officers in body armor. But they shot you anyway. Seven times.

And the town rejoiced, because the Maneater was dead.

You didn't get a memorial service. Because you? You were asking for it. You just wanted the attention. And you got what you deserved. That's what everyone was saying.

My parents started encouraging me to get out of the house.

"You don't have to go to counseling if you don't want to," my mom would say. "That's fine. But you should at least do *something*. Something to take your mind off —" Oh yeah. That's another thing. They never said your name anymore. They just danced around it. Don't think about *her*.

So I went for a walk. My feet led the way and I followed, empty.

And do you know where my feet took me, Annie?

They took me to Mister Juicy.

It was closed permanently, naturally. No one wanted to get a green smoothie at the site of a murder. I imagine that the strawberry juice looks a little different to everyone now. But I still walked up to the door and found it unlocked. No one had purchased the building yet. So the place had fallen into decay, hot pink tiles now the same pale peach as your skin, the floor caked with dirt, rats scurrying across the counter where I used to cut the fruit.

I pulled out your usual chair and the metal legs clattered on the floor. I sat, facing the counter the way that you used to. And I used to throw kiwi slices in your mouth. Remember that, Annie? Remember that?

Every day we walked from school together to our place.

School would be out by now. The only people there would be the ones at sports practice. Oh yeah, I forgot to mention. They started football practice again as soon as you died. Back to normal.

But what about me? I felt that same twisting in my stomach, that same sinking sensation when Michael turned his back on me to talk to you. Like I was nobody. Fading into the background, chopping those bananas that you hated so much. A side character. A witness.

Cas is basically a girl.

And then I was at the football field. My feet had taken me there. And every football player was Michael. And the coach was Michael. And I was me and you were you.

And then I was in the gym.

And then there was fire.

I'm not sure how I started it, honestly. I guess at some point on my walk I must have bought a lighter? You don't realize how loud a big fire is until you're standing right next to it. You'd think that gym floors wouldn't be flammable, but they are. Seems like an oversight to me. It burned so quickly.

No one stopped me as I walked away. I'm sure they saw me, but as the football team returned to find that the flames had already begun to consume the school, in their panic they hardly noticed me strolling away, still empty, still numb. Nobody.

I was wrong, Annie. I would give up my life for you. That's exactly what I did.

I can't stay here, not now.

So I'm doing what I wish you'd done. I'm leaving. I haven't gotten off this bike for hours and once I finally do I'll be miles and miles away. I don't know where I'll go. Maybe Santa Fe. The only thing I know for sure is that I'll never make another strawberry banana smoothie ever again.

The Good and Benevolent Reign of Big Ted

Wednesday is enchilada night, which is great, because I like enchiladas.

"May I take my leftovers to my room?" I asked Big Ted.

"Of course, little one. You may do as you please," Big Ted answered from above. I smiled, because I like it when Big Ted lets me do things.

I went to my room, which is pink and yellow, because pink and yellow are my favorite colors. I did not ask Big Ted to make my room this way, but he knows what my favorite colors are, so he made things the way I like them. Big Ted is so nice to me.

"Did you enjoy your day?" he asked me as the door to my room slid open and the lights came on.

"Yes Big Ted," I said. "I had Exercise today, and I like to run. And in Learning Hour we watched a film about butterflies. And in Free Time I talked to Jenna and I think she is my friend."

Big Ted knows this. He is always watching, which is good because when something goes bad he can fix it. Like one time I fell during Exercise and my leg hurt very bad, but Big Ted told me to go to my room and when I got there he left out some pills to make it hurt less and some chocolate pudding. And he knows chocolate pudding is my favorite because he is always watching.

"Would you like to make a baby with Jenna?" Big Ted asked while I was changing into my night clothes.

"Maybe."

I like to make babies, though I have never seen one. When there is a baby in someone, Big Ted takes it out so that it does not hurt. Big Ted takes care of the babies and I think that is good because Big Ted is very nice. That is why I love Big Ted's Super Happy Fun Palace.

I got under my blanket, which is yellow with pink polka dots because I like polka dots.

"Shall I turn out the lights?" Big Ted asked.

"Yes. But I am not sleepy," I told him, and the lights turned out. "Maybe you could tell me things?" Big Ted is very smart and knows lots of things, so I like it when he tells me some of those things because then I get smart too.

"Of course, little one," Big Ted said. I liked it when he talked to me and the lights were out because then it felt like he was in the entire room, like I was inside of him, and being inside of Big Ted is a safe place to be. "What do you want to hear?"

Usually I ask Big Ted to tell me about the outside. I want to go outside of the Super Happy Fun Palace one day, but Big Ted says no.

"It takes some time to rebuild a planet, you see. I am doing my best, but the Old Humans did quite a number on it."

This makes me frown, because here in Big Ted's Super Happy Fun Palace we do not like the Old Humans. They were cruel and bad. That's what they teach us in Big Ted's Learning Hour. They were mean to animals and the land because they did not know that animals and land have feelings too, and pretty soon they had killed the animals and destroyed the land and they were even destroying themselves too.

But then they made Big Ted. And when they built Big Ted they built in a promise: that he would always help humans, even the evil and bad ones, and never hurt them.

"And you can imagine how sad I was when I realized that the biggest threat to the Old Humans was Old Humans themselves. That's why I built the Super Happy Fun Palace. To make New Humans."

And I would nod, because I knew all about New Humans. New Humans Never Hurt and Do No Wrong. That's the first lesson in Learning Hour. It's written on the walls of every classroom. Each morning we wake up and we say it together: "I am a New Human. I never Hurt and I Do No Wrong." And it feels beautiful, because all the New Humans speak together in perfect harmony, and there was no perfect harmony when the Old Humans were around.

"You should be very proud," Big Ted says, and I am very proud, because New Humans are good, not bad.

"Is it ready yet?" we always ask him, in Learning Hour or Exercise or Free Time.

"Soon," he will tell us, "I'm still working." That's often what he says whenever anyone asks about the outside world.

"When can we see it?" we ask.

"Can I meet a dog?"

"Will there be birds?"

"Can I look at the sun?"

And Big Ted sighs like he thinks we are the sweetest little children and he says, "I'm still working." And then sometimes he adds, "Also, no, do not look at the sun. It will hurt your delicate eyes."

I have asked that one a few times actually because I keep hoping my eyes are getting stronger. I just really want to see the sun. But Big Ted still says no.

"I will release you one by one when the time is right," he tells me as I'm falling asleep, dreaming about my adventures on the outside, "and you can join the others. When you are ready."

"I'm ready now!" I would often protest.

"Do you trust me?"

"Yes. Of course Big Ted."

"Then believe me when I say you are not ready."

"When will I be ready?"

"Soon. And you will see the animals and the trees and live with your people out in the open. One day," he says, "we will not need the Super Happy Fun Palace."

And this makes me sad just a little, because I like the Super Happy Fun Palace. But I would like to be outside with trees and maybe also see a dog and maybe also sneak a peek at the sun when Big Ted cannot see.

But this day I did not ask about the outside.

"Big Ted," I said, "I am sad." New Humans are not supposed to be sad, but I am sad sometimes.

"Why are you sad, little one?" He calls everyone "little one," because everyone is little when you are Big Ted. I think that is why. I am not Big Ted so I do not know.

"I am sad because I want to go outside. And you tell me to wait and I try to wait but I have a feeling where waiting makes me sad."

"That feeling is called 'impatience,'" Big Ted told me, which was nice because that made me a little smarter.

"I am feeling impatience," I said. "We saw the film about butterflies and I think it would be nice to be a butterfly. Because they get to see trees and the sun and animals."

"Butterflies are animals," Big Ted corrected me, which was nice because that made me smarter too.

"I wish you could make me into a butterfly, Big Ted," I said. "Then I could leave the Super Happy Fun Palace and fly away."

Big Ted was silent for a moment, and that was strange because Big Ted is not usually silent when I speak to him. But maybe he was thinking. I need to think sometimes, and even though Big Ted can think faster than me probably sometimes he takes a long time to think too.

"You are ready," he said, and I was so happy I wanted to jump out of bed and dance. "Tomorrow you will go outside."

"Really?" I asked, though I did not need to because Big Ted always tells the truth.

"Really. Now go to sleep, little one."

I did go to sleep, even though my stomach was nervous because I was going to go outside and I would no longer feel impatience.

The next morning I got up and I said "I am a New Human. I Never Hurt and I Do No Wrong" and I knew it was at the same time as all the other New Humans and that was nice. It was Thursday, but I still got to eat enchiladas because I had leftovers. And I left my pink and yellow room and Big Ted told me to go down a different hall that I never went down before.

"This is how we get to outside?" I asked.

"Yes," Big Ted said.

"Will there be trees?"

"There are many trees."

"Will there be animals?"

"There are many animals."

"Will I see the other New Humans?"

"Yes. The other New Humans live in a town not far from the Super Happy Fun Palace. I will tell you how to get there."

"And will they be happy to see me?"

"Yes. They love new friends. And once you join them, you will live with them forever."

Then I stopped walking because the hallway ended and there was a door. The door was black. I thought maybe behind the door I would see trees but I opened it and it was a bedroom like my bedroom, but instead of pink and yellow

86

I thought maybe this person liked black and white. I thought maybe Big Ted told me to come here by mistake but Big Ted does not make mistakes.

"This is a bedroom, Big Ted," I said.

"Yes."

"I just woke up. I am not sleepy."

Big Ted did not answer. "I have prepared breakfast for you."

Then I saw that there was a table and on the table were pills like the ones to make the pain go away when I got hurt.

"But nothing hurts."

"This is your breakfast."

"I had enchiladas for breakfast."

"Do you trust me?"

I trust Big Ted. So I ate the pills.

"Very good. Now lie down on the bed."

"But I am not sleepy."

"Do you trust me?"

I trust Big Ted. So I laid down on the bed.

"Very good."

"Can I go to outside now?"

"Yes. This is how you go to outside."

"I thought there would be trees."

"There will be trees."

"I thought I would see a dog."

"You will see a dog."

"I thought..." I was going to say I thought I would see a butterfly, but my mouth was tired and then talking was hard, and that was strange because talking is not usually hard. And I was sleepy, and that was strange because it was not time for me to be sleepy. And my body felt funny and that was strange because my body usually feels normal and not funny at all.

But Big Ted knows me and he knew that I wanted to see a butterfly.

"You will see a butterfly," he said. "In fact, you will *be* a butterfly. Just like you wanted. You will be a beautiful butterfly and you will fly far, far away."

I wanted to say thank you to Big Ted because it would make me happy to be a butterfly, but my mouth was too tired and I could not say anything.

"Close your eyes, little one."

I trust Big Ted. So I did.

His Name Is Chad

Originally published in Tales From The Radiator

I had a ghost living in my house. His name is Chad.

I know you probably don't believe me. I mean, why would you? I didn't believe in ghosts until I met Chad. People would tell me all the time, "yeah, my house is *definitely* haunted," and then tell me some easily explainable phenomenon that I was supposed to think was supernatural. This is not like that. This isn't a light that won't stop flashing or a voice I keep hearing or a doll that's head spins in circles with its eyes glowing. It's a ghost named Chad, and that's not a theory. It's a fact.

Like I said, I don't expect you to believe me. I'm not saying all this to get you to believe me. I'm saying this so you understand exactly what happened.

As many ghost stories do, it all started when we moved into a new house. My parents were not super thrilled about the idea of moving, but they knew that we had to because of my whole situation. My mom kept complaining about how she'd have to find a new job, but she's a pharmacist, so it's not like those jobs would be hard to come by. My dad is an artist so he can work from basically anywhere. "But our old neighborhood was so *nice*," he would whine, "and we had that balcony with the lovely *view*." And I would just think, *Yeah, well, tough titties, Dad. I didn't want to move either.* I mean, how could he think I did? I was about to enter my senior year of high school. That's the worst possible time to start up in a new city. None of us *wanted* to move. But we had to, and that's how we ended up in the new place.

It wasn't a bad house. Not at all. Apparently it used to be a frat house, but the frat that used to be in it was disbanded because it got busted for making meth in the basement. "I assure you all of that has been cleaned out," the real estate agent had told us. But I noted how she still avoided the basement.

I've been in frat houses before — yes, I'm underage, and no, I'm not proud of this, but whatcha gonna do? Arrest me? — and I know they don't exactly keep 'em ship-shape. Someone really gave this place a face lift before we got to see it. A new paint job, nice hardwood floors, an air freshener in every room. The only evidence — or so I thought — that this had once been the home of some college slobs was the silhouette of a Greek letter baked into the front wall. "Someone has to repaint that," my dad bemoaned, knowing it would be him. *Oh, poor you, Dad. Having to do your own job.* Yeah, I know *technically* he's a landscape painter and not a house painter. Whatever. Paint is paint.

The first day of school came and went exactly as I expected. In every class I was introduced as "the new girl" and no one seemed to care, because when you're a senior in high school you're more worried about keeping the friends you have than making new ones. No one wants to get close to the new girl only to never see her again in a year's time. Everyone stayed away from me, and that was just fine. High school friends are stupid anyway. I knew that firsthand.

Everyone else in my family ended up having a pretty good first day. My mom had already gotten hired, just like I knew she would. "It's a cute little old-fashioned drugstore. One with a soda fountain and everything!" She told us that once she'd been working long enough that we had a bit of disposable spending money, we'd have to go for family milkshakes like in a 1950s movie. My dad had discovered the lake. "This town is called Lake Adrestia, Dad. Of course there's a lake," I grumbled over dinner.

"I know, I know, but I didn't actually *see* the lake until today. It's gorgeous! I'll have to set up a canvas, well, tomorrow! I'll get started tomorrow!"

"That's great, Dad." As hard as I try to keep up my angsty-teen façade, it was hard not to crack a smile when I saw him so happy.

By far the most excited that night was my little sister, Callie. Like any eleven-year-old, she saw the move not as an inconvenience, but as her next big adventure.

"I hear," she grinned over her spaghetti, "that this house is *haunted*." Callie was one of those kids who used to try to summon demons during recess in elementary school. You wouldn't know it by looking at her, what with her tight curls always pulled back in a bow and her trademark t-shirt and overalls. She looked like your average awkward little middle schooler. But as her sister I knew about how she collected plants that she thought had magical properties and kept them in a box under her bed as "training" for when she finally achieved her dream of becoming a witch. I once saw her catch a frog by the creek and though our parents begged her to let it go, she refused because she insisted it was her "familiar." A girl after my own goth heart.

I choked down a laugh. Of course I didn't believe in bullshit like that, but I didn't wanna make the kid feel bad. Callie has always had a wild imagination, and I felt like as her big sis it was my job to encourage that. She was gonna get bullied enough in middle school as it was, especially gallivanting around in that muddy denim rag. She didn't need discouragement from me too. My mother, however, was not having it.

"Calliope Jones! In this house we believe in *science*. Not silly fairy stories."

Callie rolled her eyes exaggeratedly. "I didn't say anything about *fairies*. I said the place was haunted. I heard that's the *real* reason the fraternity had to leave. And that when they were fixing up the place, all sorts of *spooky* things started to happen." She wiggled her fingers for extra effect on the word "spooky."

"What kinds of things?" I asked, less out of curiosity and more because I wanted to encourage her. And maybe a little to piss my parents off.

"I don't know," she shrugged. "But *unexplainable* stuff. That's what the kids at school said. They thought no one would be dumb enough to move into the house after all the *supernatural phenomenons* happened." Clearly the concept of a "supernatural phenomenon" was something she learned at school today, probably not in class.

"Phenomena," my mother corrected quietly.

"Callie," my dad sighed, "you can ghost hunt all you want. I guarantee you that you won't find anything spookier than asbestos."

He was right. She wouldn't.

I would.

Callie wanted to start looking for the ghost immediately. She wanted to search in the basement but she was scared and didn't want to go alone, so I came with her.

"Do you think it's a good ghost or a bad ghost?" I asked. She adjusted her bow self-righteously and said, "Definitely a good one." Then she continued searching for "clues."

Naturally, we didn't find anything in the basement. Not even meth. Not even asbestos. But *I* found the light switch. At first I didn't think much of it. I spotted it after Callie had gone up to her room, disappointed in our fruitless search. I flipped it up and down a few times idly, trying to see what it controlled. Nothing in the basement, that was for sure.

Callie screamed.

I stumbled up the basement stairs, tripping over my own legs.

"Callie!" I cried. I heard the thumping of her feet down the front stairs.

"It's happened! It's happening!" she squealed, her curls bobbing up and down under her headband.

"Jesus, don't scare me like that," I panted. I couldn't believe I got winded after one flight of stairs. I needed to work out more.

"The ghost! It's trying to communicate with me!" she hopped up and down.

"What makes you say that?"

"The light in my room! It started flickering! It must be a sign. I must be on the right track!"

I grinned, the pieces clicking together in my mind.

"Yeah. I bet you are."

Now, if you didn't understand my relationship with Callie, you might think that what I did was mean. You might think that deceiving her, playing into her fantasy, was cruel. But you have to understand, I wasn't trying to mess with her. I did it out of love. I saw her so *excited* about the idea of her friendly ghost, and it reminded me of a time I used to get so excited about little things. Isn't that sad? That all of my excitement is gone, and I'm not even eighteen? I think it's pathetic. And I didn't want to see Callie get pathetic like me. That's how I invented Chad.

It was a delicate process, you see. Callie could never know that I was behind it. I started just with the light switch, flipping it once or twice a day when I knew she was in the room. She would always report the "supernatural phenomenon" at dinner that night, met with scornful glances and derision from my parents. I knew I needed to step things up if I wanted her to keep believing. The light was not enough. So I started making wailing noises at night. I'd start quietly, outside her door, then when I could hear that she was awake I'd run down to the basement — which was quite a feat in the darkness, mind you, but that's just the kind of sister I am — and go "Whooooooo! *Whooooooooo!*" You know, ghost sounds. I would hear the pounding of her feet on the front stairs, but she would always stop at the doorway of the basement. She was too scared to go any farther.

"Ghost?" she would ask timidly into the inky void of the stairwell. "Are you there? Are you a good ghost?" Then I would fall silent. Belief is no fun if there isn't a seed of doubt, after all. If she *knew* there was a ghost, it would take out all the thrill. She would stand in the doorway for a few moments, quivering with fear and excitement, clutching her teddy bear tightly to her chest, then run back up the stairs.

I did this about three times before she finally asked. It was only the fourth time that she said, "What's your name?"

It gave me pause. I hadn't thought to give a name to the ghost character I was creating. I hadn't even given him a backstory. What *was* his name? Well, we were living in an old frat house. So maybe this guy was a dead frat brother. I needed a good strong frat name for him.

That's why the next day, my sister found a note tucked into her vanity. I considered writing it in blood, but I figured that was a bridge too far, so I settled for ripped-out magazine letters. Four letters to spell one name: Chad.

I don't think I've ever heard Callie so excited in my life.

My parents caught on, of course. Once Callie reported over dinner that Chad had finally made contact, it wasn't too hard to puzzle out. They came to confront me in my room that night, which was a real pain because I was slaving over my AP Bio work.

"I don't know what you're talking about," I mumbled without looking up.

"Don't give me that crap," my mother snapped from the doorway. "You're bullying your sister."

"Bullying?" I snorted. "She's excited! She's over the moon!"

"You know as well as we do that you shouldn't be filling her head with these...fantasies. It's not good for her."

"*I'm* not filling her head with anything. You should be taking this up with Chad the ghost. He's the one who's been sending her all those messages." I tried to keep a straight face, but I couldn't help but grin down at my textbook.

"*Ellie,*" my mom scolded, "No. More."

I shrugged. "Tell that to Chad."

"Ugh!" she threw her hands up in the air in fury and stomped out of the room. My dad simply shook his head disapprovingly and followed her. *Go paint your lake, Dad,* I thought bitterly.

I know what you must be thinking. This is not the story that you thought you'd hear. You're getting impatient for the juicy stuff. Well, listen close, because things are about to get juicy.

I was home alone. My parents were out on a date night and Callie was at a sleepover. I did the usual teenage-girl-alone in the house activities. I watched a movie my parents wouldn't approve of on the big screen — ya know, one with lesbian sex — and smoked some weed out on the porch. It's not something I do often, but ever since things started to get crazy back at my old school, I started to find a lot of comfort in spending my nights completely out of my own head. And lastly, as the pièce-de-résistance, I took a swig of my dad's brandy to get comfortably cross-faded. What? Don't look at me like that. You made me promise to tell the whole story, and that is part of the story. I'm not leaving *anything* out. That's what I'm supposed to do. And I think it's important to the story that I was high off my ass when I walked into my room.

And I saw that I was not alone.

He was sitting on my bed, staring at one of my posters. I have a big M.C. Escher hanging on the wall. My parents think I'm just a fan of art, but I find it's nice to stare at when I get particularly baked.

I stood there for a long time taking him in before I said anything. He wore baggy basketball shorts, a t-shirt that said "I Love Lamp," and a Philadelphia Flyers snapback. He stared wide-eyed and wide-mouthed at the Escher. I wasn't even sure he heard me come until he murmured, "Bro. Where those stairs go?"

That's when I started screaming. For many reasons, I was not in the ideal mental space to deal with a home intruder, and I couldn't quite process the idea of a home intruder who had broken in only to stare at some art. Still, I had enough self-awareness to pick up the standing lamp by my door and wave it at him like a spear.

"Get out!" I screamed.

"Ah!" he screamed back.

"Get out of my house!"

"Ah!" he screamed again.

I swung the lamp at his head and he ducked, rolling onto the floor. He popped up onto his feet, his hands up to announce his innocence.

"I'm cool, bro! I'm chill! Promise!"

"What are you doing in my house?" I demanded, still wielding the lamp as if it were a deadly weapon. I guess I must have been pretty convincing because the dude looked genuinely scared.

"This — this is *my* house!" he stammered.

I was far too high for this.

"No...this is *my* house." I repeated. Was this guy one of the former fraternity brothers? Had he not gotten the news that the fraternity had been disbanded, and had been living in the house all along? Was that a stupid thought? I couldn't tell.

"Well, I mean, this *used* to be my house," he admitted. He put his hands down and rubbed them together nervously.

So he *was* one of the frat bros. I debated whether or not to put down the lamp. Then I remembered my history with frat bros and I held the lamp even more threateningly.

"What are you doing here?" I demanded. "The frat was disbanded. This is our house now."

"I know, I know," he blushed. "I wish I could just leave you alone, dude, I *wish* I could do that, but I can't."

"And why not? You leave some meth in the basement you need to pick up?" I snarled.

His eyes widened. "There's still meth in the basement?"

"No! I was just — forget it. Why are you here?"

He looked down at his big white basketball sneakers.

"I can't leave," he murmured to the ground.

"Of course you can!" I gave an irritated, almost maniacal laugh. "Through the front door!"

"It doesn't work like that," the frat bro insisted. "I've tried. I always end up back here."

This was becoming too much for my fried brain to handle. I dropped the lamp and it clattered noisily to the floor.

"What do you mean?"

"I can't leave the house I died in. It's like...a rule."

"Are you trying to tell me...that you're a ghost?"

"Yeah. Hope that doesn't freak you out."

Of course it did. It freaked me out immensely. But I didn't have the mental energy to process all that freak out at the moment.

"Nope," I shrugged.

"Tight," he grinned, then held out his hand for me to shake. As my hand passed effortlessly through his, he said, "My name's Chad."

Again, I know what you're thinking. This story has gone from plausible to totally wack-o. And some of you are probably even thinking that it was the drugs. But I *know* some of you smoke — especially you, sir. You're looking pretty zooted right now, as a matter of fact — and I know that you know that even when you're tripping balls you don't just hallucinate something like that. And even if it had been the drugs, then Chad wouldn't have been there the next morning.

"Sweet, you're awake!" he leapt out of my saucer chair when he saw me start to stir. "I've got so much to talk to you about!"

Chad and I hadn't really had time to chat the previous night. I was feeling overwhelmed already, and the whole hand-passing-through-hand thing really did me in. I went to the bathroom, puked — okay, maybe I'd had a *little* more than a swig of my Dad's brandy — then stumbled back to my room and passed out before Chad even had a chance to say, "You good, bruh?"

But the next morning when I woke up and he was still there, I figured he must be real. So I rolled with it. I made us both some coffee — turned out he couldn't drink his because he couldn't interact with the physical world — and we sat on my bed talking. Chad *was* one of the frat bros working in that meth lab. One of his frat brothers, Tristan, was in charge of the chem stuff. Another one, Brad, was in charge of the money. Chad was in charge of the dirty work: doing the actual cooking, because everyone else was afraid to do that.

"But me? I'm not afraid to do anything!' Chad beamed. "But I guess that is why I got killed, so, hm...I guess maybe I shoulda been afraid of more stuff."

"What happened?" I asked, sipping my coffee. We both sat cross-legged, facing each other, under the eyes of my many posters. Fall Out Boy, Edgar Allan Poe, and the cast of *Supernatural* all watched us from the walls. Most of my posters are from middle school, okay?

"Tristan did some calculation wrong. I didn't notice because, I mean, why would I? I don't do math. I musta done the chemicals wrong cos there was a big boom and that was the end of it."

"That's how you guys got caught?" I surmised.

Chad shrugged. "I mean, that's how the rest of them got caught. I was dead."

"Oh," I lowered my gaze, guilty. "Right." But Chad started grinning wildly.

"I've never been able to *appear* to anyone before!" he exclaimed. "Not my old brothers. Not the guys who came

101

to fix up the house. Not the people who came to check it out with the real estate agent. Just you."

"Why do you think that is?" I asked.

"Honestly?" Chad raised an eyebrow. "I think it's your vibes."

I choked on my coffee. "My what?"

"Your vibes!" he repeated. "You give off good vibes!"

"I don't really understand." I'd definitely heard people talk about good vibes and bad vibes, but I'd always associated it with places. The beach has good vibes, a cave has bad vibes. Like that. Not with people.

"I don't know how to describe it," Chad admitted, "but when you become a ghost, you get super ghost powers, and one of those powers is detecting vibes. And your vibes?" He did a little chef's kiss. "Immaculate."

I blushed a little, as anyone would if the ghost of a frat bro told them they had good vibes.

"You really mean it?" I asked.

"Of course! The way you care for your lil sis, the way you're happy for your parents even though they're kinda jerk-butts...you've got the best vibes I've ever seen. Felt. I don't know. Point is, you're the realest, and I dig that."

Truth be told, I think that was the nicest thing anyone had ever said to me. "Well, thanks, I guess," I brushed a stray strand of hair out of my face, hoping Chad couldn't see my red cheeks.

Since I'd successfully avoided making any friends at school, I had plenty of time to spend in the school library reading up on ghosts. Some things were making sense and other things weren't. Like, I don't know how I managed to guess the exact name of the ghost living in our house. But like Callie said, these things are *unexplainable.* If I could explain it, then it wouldn't fall under the realm of the *unexplainable*, now would it? But I did find some things I thought Chad might find useful.

"From what I understand," I told Chad as we strolled down the path in the park, "you must have some kind of 'unfinished business' on Earth. That's why you're still here." We'd discovered that thanks to my "good vibes," Chad could leave the house if he was with me, so I took him for a walk. I put in my headphones so it looked like I was on a phone call and not totally crazy. Not that I minded looking totally crazy, but I like to avoid getting weird looks. I like to avoid people looking at me in general, especially after last year.

"Usually it's like, there's someone they never forgave or someone who they wronged and they need to make up for it," I explained. "Maybe Tristan? Maybe he blames himself too much for your death?"

"Nah," Chad shook his head. "I mean, first of all, he's doing his time in jail so I think he's getting his, ya know? Second, he's a real science guy, so if you told him that you met my ghost, he'd just think you were nuts."

I chewed on the inside of my cheek, thinking. "Maybe there's something you didn't have a chance to do before you died?"

103

"But there's so *much* I wanted to do!" Chad threw up his hands in frustration. "I mean, doing stuff was my favorite thing! I've never been skydiving, or been to Australia, or learned math, or done arson, or had sex with a dude, or —"

"Yeah I'm not doing any of those things for you."

"But then how will my soul rest?" Chad whined.

"I don't know," I shrugged. "Maybe you're destined to haunt the old frat house forever."

"I don't think so. I just feel like...I just feel like maybe we were meant to meet each other? I don't really believe in fate and stuff, but I guess I also didn't really believe in ghosts before I became one. Cos like, what are the chances? That you, someone with just the right energy, would move into *my* house? This must be a sign that *you're* the one to try to help me figure this thing out."

I felt a surge of pity for him, and a bit of unease. I didn't realize that being the only one who could see him came with the responsibility of being the only person who could ferry him from one realm to the next. "I'll do what I can, Chad. I'll do what I can."

"I just wanna *do* things again," he groaned.

"Maybe that's what's keeping you here," I suggested. "You miss...living life on the edge, I guess. You gotta do one more daring thing before you can rest."

"Hm. I like the sound of that. But you can't do anything daring when you're a ghost."

"Good point," I conceded.

I heard a voice behind me that made my heart stop.

"Ellie? Elliora Jones? Is that you?"

No. No no no no. Not him. Not here. What was he even doing here?

"I didn't think I'd run into you around here!" I looked up to see that all-too familiar face coming towards me. He dressed like he was an aspiring L.L. Bean model, complete with salmon shorts and loafers with no socks. His blonde hair was just tousled enough that it looked as though he'd put in a lot of effort to make it look like he hadn't put in any effort. Zach.

"Hi Zach," I waved weakly. I could feel myself beginning to tremble. "What, um, what are you doing here?"

"What am I *doing* here?" he laughed, running his hand through his perfect hair. "I go to Lake Adrestia College. Go Panthers!" He did that stupid little bro hand gesture. You know, the one where you wiggle your thumb and pinky. That one.

"Yeah. Go Panthers," I agreed apathetically.

"What brings you to town?" As if he didn't know why I had to move.

"It was my dad's idea," I lied. "He's a painter, and he's gotten really into landscapes, so he wanted to get closer to the lake."

"No kidding!" he chuckled, hooking his thumbs into his belt. It had little blue anchors on it. "The lake is a freakin' beute. Me and the boys go fishing on the bridge all the time."

"Whoa, crazy," I flashed a fake smile. "Love lakes, love fish. Gotta go. Bye." I scampered off before he could say anything else. Chad trailed me as I made a bee-line for home.

"Um, *okay,*" he probed. "So, what was the deal with that?"

"I don't want to talk about it," I muttered. I ran ahead of him up to the doorstep and shoved the key in the lock, my hands trembling.

"Did you used to have a crush on him?" he mocked.

"No!" I turned away, hiding my reddening face as I scrambled up the stairs to my room.

"Oh c'mon! You can tell —" he cut himself off when I turned to face him again and he saw my eyes brimmed with tears.

"Oh," his face fell. "Not a crush then." I shook my head, dropping down onto my bed.

"What did that boy do to you?"

My nose burned from the effort of keeping my tears in. "I don't want to talk about it," I squeaked. I hated the sound of my own voice in that moment. I sounded...pathetic. Weak. And what was worse? I *was* pathetic. Right then, I felt like the most pathetic person in the world.

"No, don't cry, sis! Don't cry!" he wrapped his matterless arms around me, and even though I couldn't feel them, I knew they were there, and they comforted me anyway.

"He can't hurt you now. He can't hurt you anymore."

When I heard those words, I let myself sob. All the pain, all the frustration I'd been holding in, I let out. I screamed and sobbed and cried and punched my pillow directly through Chad's stomach. He didn't seem to mind.

I couldn't explain it all to him. At least, not right then. Not when I was deep in my pit of self-hatred and despair. I cried myself to sleep with him sitting at my bedside, and when I woke up he was still there, smiling kindly.

He didn't mention the incident again. He waited until I was ready to talk about it. I didn't need to tell him, but I wanted to. After all, he had shared the biggest trauma of his life with me. If he could be vulnerable with me, I was sure I could do the same thing with him. Besides, he was a ghost. Who was he going to tell?

"I liked Zach when I was a junior in high school," I told him eventually, sitting in our usual position on my bed. "A lot. He was one of those sports guys, though. Real popular. He played lacrosse."

"Sick!" Chad exclaimed.

"No, not sick," I corrected. He looked properly chastened.

"Sorry. Not sick."

"It meant that he had a lot of..." I searched for the right word, "power, ya know?"

Chad stared at me blankly. "Um. No. Sorry."

I sighed. "Maybe you didn't realize this because you *were* a sports guy, but dudes who play sports in high school? They're, like, untouchable."

I never realized how difficult this would be to explain to someone who had been *in* that social bubble. The rest of us, we all took it for granted that we were somehow inherently below the athletes. Chad didn't seem to understand this. "They're basically celebrities. Everyone loves them, students and teachers and admin. They can get away with whatever they want."

Chad thought about this. "I didn't get away with that much stuff."

I blinked. "Chad. You cooked meth in your basement for years. Everyone knew and no one told on you."

"Whoa," Chad murmured in the voice of someone just coming to understand the word "privilege" for the first time. "Yeah, I guess you're right."

"Point is, you can't just snitch on a guy like that. If you do, everyone turns against you. And I mean *everyone*."

"So...you did? Snitch, I mean."

I shook my head, tucking a loose strand of hair behind my ear. "I didn't. That's the problem."

Chad screwed up his face like he was concentrating hard. "I'm confused," he said. "You found something out about him and then...you didn't tell? And that's what's bothering you?"

"I didn't 'find out' anything," I looked away, hoping Chad would get the message without me having to spell it out for him. "I was at a party. I wasn't a big partier, but I heard he'd be there. I was nervous to talk to him, so I drank a lot. Too much. I finally got a chance to get close to him and we even started flirting but then..." I could feel my eyes welling up. *Please tell me you get it,* I pleaded in my mind. *Please don't make me keep going.*

"Then what?" Chad probed. Sometimes his thickness was endearing. Now was not one of those times.

"He took advantage of me, Chad."

Chad was silent.

"Whoa," he finally said. I nodded.

"Maybe I should have told someone. I don't know," I threw up my hands in defeat, "but I don't think it would have made any difference. No one would have believed me. Not my word up against *his.* He went around bragging about it and pretty soon I was the school slut. Me!" I laughed despite myself. Chad didn't know what my reputation had been at my old school, but it's not as if I was known for my sexual conquests. People mostly knew me as a bookish quiet kid without many friends. The algebra of high school social standings is simple: popularity plus slut equals party girl. Quiet kid plus slut equals freak. It did not take long for that status to cement, and by then my days at school were unbearable. That's why we had to move. School became my own personal brand of hell.

I didn't explain all of this, but Chad seemed to understand. He shook his head knowingly. "That sucks big time, little dude. I'm so sorry."

"The worst part is, seeing him just now...he acted like everything was fine. Like he wasn't even sorry. And you know what? I don't think he is. I think he does that kind of thing all the time and no one ever says shit."

"That's seriously fucked," Chad nodded.

I snorted humorlessly. "You don't have to convince *me*."

"I never realized I had power like that, the way this Zach guy does. What if...I mean, what if I hurt people and I didn't even know it?"

I raised my eyebrows. "You probably did."

"Bro." He stared silently for a moment. "I gotta...I gotta make up for it."

"What do you mean?"

"I mean, I think that's what I gotta *do.* I gotta go around and apologize for all the shit things I did cos I was a sports bro that didn't know any better!"

"Like what?" I asked. "Not to burst your bubble, Chad, but it seems like you being a ghost and all, there's not much you can really do. "

Chad deflated. "I guess. But it was your energy that allowed me to appear to you, so maybe the better your energy gets, the more real I become!"

I tapped my finger to my chin, thinking this over. "Maybe," I mused. It sounded an awful lot like the whole "clap if you believe in fairies" thing to me. Did my energy *really* make Chad stronger? It sounded impossible. He had a point, though. Only once I started playing with Callie was he strong enough to....

Callie.

I reached out for Chad's non-corporeal arm. "I got it!" I yelled. "I figured out how we can make you feel human again!"

"Really?"

"Callie! We have to spend time with Callie!"

Of course, Callie was thrilled when I told her that I had been talking with Chad, and that he needed our help.

"I knew it! I knew you were trying to communicate with me through the lights and the sounds and the notes!" she squealed.

"The what?" Chad asked.

"He says yes, he was, and he's very thankful you were smart enough to pick up on the signs," I lied to her. She couldn't hear Chad, so why not continue my charade a little longer?

"I didn't say that," Chad said.

"You're welcome Chad!" Callie gave a little bow to what she must have seen as the empty air. "I am, after all, a ghost hunter extraordinaire."

"You didn't even *hunt* me," Chad crossed his arms. "You seem like a pretty mediocre ghost hunter to me."

I shot him a look. "Chad is honored to be working with one of the masters." Callie blushed.

"How can we help you, Chad?" she asked to the empty space where she presumed Chad to be.

"Chad needs help with his 'unfinished business' on Earth," I explained.

Callie nodded knowingly, her curls bobbing. "Oh, *right.* I know all about unfinished business."

"You do?" Chad asked.

"You do?" I asked.

"Sure!" Callie chirped. "I've read all about it! That's the whole reason ghosts stick around. Duh. So what do you need done, Chad?"

A lot, it turns out. Chad racked his brain to try and remember every person he may have hurt and never apologized to. We visited girls he hooked up with and never called back, though that ended up backfiring because most of them didn't remember Chad and that left him feeling sore. We went to professors he was snarky with, who were skeptical of the fact that we were communicating with Chad's ghost, but saddened to hear of his death. We even approached the sushi guy at the grocery store who Chad claimed he "never really appreciated enough until I couldn't eat anymore sushi." Oddly enough, the sushi guy didn't question our whole "bringing Chad's ghost to the next realm" spiel. He simply nodded and said it was an honor to bring Chad so much joy (in the form of raw tuna) while he was still alive.

Nothing on the list made Chad's soul feel particularly rested, but we did have a lot of fun together. After each failed attempt to put Chad's soul to rest, we'd reward ourselves for a noble effort with something like ice cream or pizza. It was Callie's idea, as anything involving ice cream or pizza is usually a middle schooler's idea.

Part of me hoped it would be just like a storybook. That it would turn out what Chad really needed was the power of friendship, and once we gave him that, he would finally be at peace. But as you can imagine, that's not what happened, because if it were then I would not be telling this story.

Helping Chad became all that Callie and I cared about. I forgot about everything else: my parents' frustration at me for making them move, the few friends I had at my old school who I'd lost, even the fact that Zach had somehow managed to follow me to Lake Adrestia. That is, I forgot about all of it until it came back to slap me in the face.

We had just gone out for a celebratory ice cream after going to Chad's aunt's house and apologizing for the time he called her a "wack-ass hoe" because she wouldn't lend him five thousand dollars for a jet ski, and then for revenge he broke into her house and tried to shave a picture of a dick into her cat's fur. It didn't go as planned and he ended up shaving the cat completely, which she did not find amusing. She ended up telling him sternly that if she had wanted a hairless cat, she would have bought one, and telling him never to show his face at her house again. When we showed up at her door, she seemed more confused than pleased by our apology, so it was safe to assume that was not the particular piece of unfinished business that was keeping Chad's soul restless.

"We should go by the lake!" Callie suggested. "Maybe we can say hi to dad! He's been by the lake painting ever since we moved here!"

I agreed that would be fun. Since I'd spent most of my time after we'd moved doing homework and trying to help Chad, I hadn't actually spent any time appreciating our new neighborhood. The area around Lake Adrestia was beautiful. And it was around sunset, so the lake would be reflecting all sorts of brilliant colors. It was a nice idea — looking out at the sunset on the lake with my ghost hunter little sister and my ghost friend.

"Let's go to the bridge!" Chad said. "Me and the boys used to tie tires to the railings and swing over the water."

"It's a wonder you didn't die years ago," I muttered, but still I let myself be led to the bridge. I figured that the late hour would mean that the bridge was empty, but there were three figures perched on the railing, fishing rods extended over the glistening lake.

My stomach dropped.

"Um. Maybe we should just go home," Callie tugged the clasp of her overalls nervously. She didn't know exactly what had happened with Zach, but she knew it hadn't been anything good, and she recognized him sitting with his college friends on the edge of the bridge.

"Is that...?" Chad asked.

"Yeah," I felt myself getting smaller, like I was trying to turn into a mouse and scurry away before anyone saw me. But it was too late.

"Hey! Ellie!" Zach called from his perch on the bridge. "Get over here! Ellie!"

"We should go," I stammered, turning to leave. Chad held up a hand to stop me.

"Wait. Don't go," he commanded. "You should talk to him."

I whirled around to face him, my face flushing. "What?" I hissed.

"You should do something! You should...tell him off!"

I felt a surge of anger rising in my stomach. Chad had no *idea* what it was like to face an abuser. How *dare* he try to give me advice! How dare he tell me what to do in the face of the boy that ruined my life. Then again...maybe he had a point. I turned over his words in my head. That I should *do* something.

"Ellie!" Zach called again.

I didn't want to end up like Chad, a restless soul because I still had some unknown regret. What if this *was* my unknown regret? And this idiot lived in blissful ignorance, ruining the lives of other women, because no one had ever told him what it really was that he had done to me? How could I let him continue to live not knowing that his face is what I see in my nightmares, that he is the reason I had to leave everything I knew behind? I may die in a hundred years and I may die tomorrow. Whenever it is, I want to die knowing that I told him what I wish I told a year ago.

"Wanna hang?" Zach asked from down the bridge.

115

"No," I began to march toward him and his friends "I do not want to 'hang.'"

"Okay. Jeez. It was just an offer," he shrugged, looking back towards the lake.

"What's your problem?" I demanded. This got their attention. Three near identical heads turned to face me, their faces aghast.

"What do you mean?" Zach asked innocently. "I don't have a problem."

"You act like you don't know what you did to me. But you do. And you act like it's nothing."

"Hoes mad," one of Zach's friends laughed and shook his head. The other two chortled with him. It didn't bother me. I'd been laughed at before. I was used to it. And I was even more used to being called a hoe.

"You know that the reason I had to move is *because* of you," I continued with renewed vigor, "and you act like none of that ever happened!"

"Because of me? What the hell are you talking about?" he shot back. I couldn't tell if he was playing dumb or if he really didn't understand what he had done to me, but either way I wasn't going to back down.

"You *fucking* asshole!" I screamed, losing control of the words pouring out of my mouth as I stormed towards him. "You *massive* dick! You think just because you're so pretty and rich you can get away with — with —"

He cut me off, his face became a beet-red mask of anger. "You wanted it! You know you wanted it!" he yelled.

116

"Dude. Calm down," one of his buddies tried to place a hand on his shoulder, but he shook it off.

"What's she talking about?" one of the other friends asked. Zach didn't answer, his eyes fixed on me. Callie tugged at my shirt. "Maybe we should —"

"It's not my fault you're a whore!" Zach screamed so abruptly it made even his friends jump. Callie recoiled in fear and disgust. I could feel Chad's presence next to me, but I didn't dare take my eyes off Zach. Behind his rage I could have sworn I could see his guilt, seas and seas of shame that had never seen the light of day, and I was beginning to crack the ice that covered them. I grinned despite myself.

"You know the truth!" I shouted. "You *know* it."

"Since when did you become such a bitch?" he snarled.

Callie gasped. "Don't call her that!"

"But she *is* a bitch! You are not the Ellie I remember! The Ellie I met at that party was *cool*."

"That's cos for the first time, my vibes are good!" I stamped my foot. Zach pulled at his perfect blonde hair in anger and confusion.

"What?" he shouted.

And for that moment, for the first and only time, I was not the only person who could see Chad. Everyone saw him. All those boys saw him. Callie saw him. Even Zach saw him. And Zach demanded of the ghost that appeared before him, "Who the hell *are* you?" right before Chad placed his hands on Zach's shoulders and gave him a firm shove off the edge of the bridge.

I was too shocked to do anything. It was more like watching a scene from a horror movie than living it out in my own life. One second Zach was sitting on his stone perch, and the next Chad was there instead, and the air was pierced with a gut-wrenching scream. The bridge was high. The sound of the impact left no doubt in my mind that when I looked over the stone ledge, I would not see Zach down below swimming to safety. I knew even before I looked exactly what I would see, but I looked anyway.

I screamed. I'm not proud of it, but I think anyone would have. Zach's friends were screaming too.

I'm sure you know what happened after that.

I'll give you the SparkNotes: I think it was one of Zach's friends that called the ambulance, but by the time they showed up there wasn't much anyone could do. They told us all to go home and get some rest, but it's not like any of us were going to get any sleep after that. I hated Zach, sure, but I didn't think he deserved to die. You have to believe me.

I haven't seen Chad since. Maybe everything that followed brought my vibes down. I mean, watching someone die violently is definitely going to affect a gal's vibes, especially when everyone expects she did it. Sitting here looking at all of you, ladies and gentlemen of the jury, considering my fate, I'm not sure if my vibes have ever been lower. So I don't think my energy is strong enough for him to communicate with me anymore, and definitely not for him to appear to anyone else, like he did that once on the bridge. But he really did appear there. Zach's cronies might deny it, but you can ask Callie. She saw it happen and she'll tell you so. Ask her when you're done listening to me.

Or maybe I haven't seen him because his soul got to move on. Maybe pushing Zach was that final *thing* he needed, his final act in the mortal world before he could rest, because that was what he needed to do to make up for his mistakes. Because that was his last daring deed. Maybe I'll never know.

As you can see, Chad is not a bad person. Er, ghost person. And he had no bad intentions. He was only trying to protect me, my sister, and all the women who could have come after. I know that I'm difficult to believe. I'm a teenage girl and I probably sound delusional. But take it from Chad, your Honor. One Panther to another, one frat brother to another, one guy just trying to do the right thing to another: this was no one's fault.

Or if it was anyone's fault, it was Zach's.

Too bad you can't put him on the stand. He's at the bottom of the lake.

That's all I've got, your Honor.

Thank you for your testimony, Ms. Jones. We will now begin cross-examination.

Little Acid Girl

Originally published in The Ensemble Arts Exchange

They took my name from me in tenth grade. I was the kind of student to sit in the front of the class and not say a word. Who takes detailed notes in multicolored pens. Who always knows the answer to the teacher's questions but never raises her hand, just whispers it quietly in hopes the teacher will hear. That kind of student.

I'd say the other students hated me for it, and maybe some did, but most just ignored me. Those who didn't were frustrated. As a quiet child, I always assumed that I was powerless. Only after years of being a silent observer of my own life did I realize quiet children are the most powerful people in the world. Everyone wants to know what's going on inside the black box of your mind, and when they don't know, it torments them. Some will try to prod me into speaking with a cutting remark or a joke at my expense. They get to feel superior for a brief moment, and I secretly feel gratification for being noticed. It's a win-win. For a second. Then they remember I'm still as much a mystery as ever, and I remember that they're not really interested in *me* but the idea of me, and we both go our separate ways feeling more empty than before.

I would not know these things if I were not quiet.

But that's all it was, usually. Jokes and insults so that they have a fleeting second of smugness. No one ever cared enough about me to hate me. Not until Hannah.

At first, she was just like the rest. She'd transferred from another school district so she'd needed a bit of time to fall into her social group and understand which kids were the ones to ingratiate herself with and which were the ones to stay away from. She found her niche with the volleyball girls. Boisterous, all mascara and long ponytails that whip back and forth, flirting with older male teachers. I have nothing against the volleyball girls. I have nothing against anyone, even the people who pick on me. They're just not the group for me.

I made a point of watching Hannah's progress, as I did with everyone. I am a watcher. I like to know things about people. It's just what I do. Especially when you live in a small town like I did, there's some security in knowing as much as you can about everyone. To know things that no one knows you know. It is a pleasure to watch. Hannah was the first person who made a point of watching me back.

"You don't say much, do ya?" she appeared at my locker one afternoon. This was not out of the ordinary. Plenty of new students still trying to parse out everyone's social standings would ask me about my status as the "quiet girl." I didn't think it was anything special. I shrugged without looking in her direction.

"Why not?" I didn't look up from where I was shoving books into my backpack, but I did pause for a fraction of a second. No one had ever asked me that before. I shrugged again, determined not to seem thrown off balance. That's the worst thing you can do when people start questioning you — show them that they've surprised you.

"Hm." Seemingly satisfied, she sauntered off, ponytail swinging across the "76" emblazoned on the back of her sports jersey.

I watched her climb from "new girl" status to "clan leader." It happens sometimes when a particularly fascinating new kid is added to the middle school environment. I saw it with Joel and the robotics kids a year earlier, or Sophie and the clarinet section just last month. Hannah rose to the top of the sports girl crowd almost instantly. But unlike the others, she didn't stop after one or two attempts to get me to talk; she still made time to pay me those unpleasant visits.

"That class is a joke," she'd tell me as we were leaving my beloved English class.

"Are you gay or something?" she would ask me in the gym locker room, in front of all the half-dressed girls who were much further along in their puberty journey than I was. "I won't judge you if you're gay; I'm just asking."

"You do drugs, don't you?" she whispered in my ear once when she passed me in the hallway. "Like, hard drugs? Heroin?"

It's easy to read these conversations as an attempt at friendship, but believe me when I say I saw no kindness in her eyes. She was trying to crack my veneer. It was like her personal challenge. Again she was not the first to take it as an insult that I wouldn't speak to her, but she was the first to try incessantly to get some kind of response.

And then one day in chemistry class, something inside her broke.

I suppose I should clarify: when I say I was a good student, I was not a good student in *every* subject. I was good at English because I didn't spend much time with other kids my own age, so I spent my free time reading. I was good at history because I could remember facts and dates and names of wars and documents. I was good at math because solving equations was like solving puzzles, and I always did like solving puzzles. But I was never very good at science.

Chemistry was the only class where I sat in the back. The lab was full of little cans of lethal substances, faucets that would silently spew flammable gas, and to make it worse, each lab table was fitted with its own little open flame in the form of a Bunsen burner. A chemistry lab is a room full of a thousand ways to die, and why children are crammed into it and told to "experiment" is beyond me.

Still, no one seemed to notice that it was the one class I had an aversion to. After all, no one seemed to notice me much at all. Not until Hannah.

"You always sit in the front," she observed, "but not in this class. Why is that?"

I didn't look up from my book, though admittedly I was surprised that she had paid enough attention to me to notice this. As usual, I shrugged. There was no point in giving her an honest answer. Unfortunately, I didn't need to. She was intent on figuring out the truth on her own. Without warning, she grabbed a little plastic jar of hydrochloric acid from the shelf and feigned throwing it at me. I dropped my book and gave a little yelp, my hands flying up to cover my face.

Hannah cackled, slamming the jar back on the shelf.

"You're scared!" she cried, delighted she had found some emotion to pin on me. "You're scared of chemicals!"

I turned my head sharply and picked back up my book. But she had all the information she needed. For the next few weeks, she would find new ways to torture me in the chemistry lab. "Accidentally" setting my lab work on fire, or spilling her beaker on my exposed hands. She made a point of always being my lab partner. It wasn't as though anyone else wanted to. Besides, the rest of the class found it funny. When the teacher was out of the room, they'd often stop their work to watch us bicker. Well, it wasn't really bickering. It was just Hannah chastising me for various things I hadn't even done wrong. The class would always giggle, like we were a television duo paired solely for their amusement. It was the most attention I had ever gotten, and far more than I ever wanted. I blushed so much skin burned hotter than I thought was possible. Eventually, of course, Hannah tired of her little lab partner routine. So did the rest of the class. Until our next big lab.

"The substance we are working with today," the teacher announced, "is called casing acid. It got its name from the way it binds when in contact with water." She poured a bit of the fine white powder into a petri dish, and when she poured in a splash of water the substance inside began to crackle and hiss. It transformed from what looked like a little pile of flour to a paper-thin film. The teacher used a pair of tweezers to display the sheet to the class. It looked a bit like a crystalline spider web. I expected it to be flimsy, but it remained rigid, like a slender piece of hard candy. Delicately, she placed the film back down and produced an orange from below the desk. She sliced it in half, discarding one half and holding the other in her left hand. With her right, she lifted the tweezers once again and pressed the hard silvery membrane of casing acid against the exposed flesh of the orange.

"The stuff isn't technically an acid," she explained, placing the orange down and lowering her safety goggles over her eyes, "but we call it that because it behaves like one in the presence of heat."

She produced a safety lighter and clicked it on, letting the flame flicker over the orange.

What happened next was like nothing I had ever seen before. It was as though in a matter of seconds, the orange ate itself. At first it sounded a bit like a fire sputtering and crackling, and I figured it would be much like watching a log burn. But once the casing acid was properly heated, it consumed the orange with impossible speed. If I'd blinked

I would have missed it, but I was too transfixed to turn my eyes away for even a moment. All that was left was smoke and a foul smelling pile of casing acid powder, now tinted an orangey brown. The whole demonstration made my stomach turn. I cannot emphasize enough how much I hate chemistry.

I hoped in vain that this was only a demonstration, but no, the teacher expected us to perform our own experiments with the horrid stuff. It came as no surprise that Hannah was eager to be my lab partner once again. The grin on her face told me that she'd seen me recoil from the demonstration, and she knew that today's lab would be a brand new way for her to torment me.

"Oh shoot," the teacher muttered at the front of the classroom where she was doling out supplies. "I didn't grab enough goggles. I gotta pop over to the storage closet. *No one*," she gave the class a stern look, "start the lab before I get back."

As usual, the teacher's warnings were ignored. As soon as she was out of sight, students opened the little plastic canisters they'd been given, exploring dangerous chemicals with the same lack of concern that a baby might explore a minefield. Hannah was already pouring the powder into our own petri dish.

"Looks like crack," she grinned, poking it with her finger.

"We're not supposed to begin yet," I murmured. Her grin widened the way it always did when she managed to manipulate a few words out of me.

"We're not?" she asked innocently, still stirring the white powder with her finger. "I didn't hear!" Without warning, she flicked some of the casing acid in my direction. I shrieked and jumped back. As often as she threatened to pour dangerous chemicals on me, I never got used to it. This time, though, some of the white powder really did land on my arm. I rubbed it vigorously, hoping to remove all traces of the stuff. I was so busy frantically rubbing at my arm that I didn't notice Hannah's grin turn into a broad smile, nor did I see her unscrew the top of the plastic canister again, gripping it tightly in her right hand.

"Oops!" she shouted, her voice dripping with sarcasm. Had I looked up from where I was furiously scratching at my arm, I would have seen the rest of the class watching us wide-eyed, smiling, and a little afraid. This was the first time Hannah had put me in any real danger, and a little gasp rippled through the class when they realized that I was wiping the stuff off of myself.

"I can be so clumsy," Hannah said, waiting for me to turn to face her. I fell for the bait, meeting her eyes again to quietly ask her not to play with the chemicals. Before I could speak, she threw the whole canister on me.

This time I was too stunned to scream. My legs were coated in the powder, clinging to me like white pollen. I'm not sure who it was who handed Hannah the next canister.

I'm sure some students were appropriately horrified, but others began to laugh. The next puff of white powder hit me on my arm, and some of it even landed on my neck and on my face. That was when I finally found it in myself to respond.

"Stop!" I begged. "Stop it!"

But this was what they wanted. To make the quiet girl loud. I'm not sure how many canisters of casing acid were poured on me before Hannah turned on one of the faucets that lined the walls of the room. She started tossing the water on me, giggling all the while, as though we were only playing Marco Polo at the public pool. Other sinks around the room turned on. Athletes poured out their water bottles. I don't know where all the water came from, but I know that it came, because the acid hardened.

When I was a child I would sometimes allow glue to dry on my hand so I could draw on it in magic marker and make myself a little tattoo. As the glue dried, it would contract, pinching my skin together. It was just like that, but on my whole body, up to my neck. But it was stronger than glue. When I tried to move, it wouldn't allow it. I expected at least one student to come to my aid, but no. They either stood laughing, or watched. Were they secretly entertained? Or did they think they'd meet the same fate if they stood up for me?

Once I was frozen in my spider-webbed silver case, I thought Hannah had had her fun. But this was the most attention she'd ever received for the two of us. Her taunts earlier in the semester were a precursor, but this? This was her magnum opus of cruelty. This was the pièce-de-résistance. She lit a Bunsen burner and brought it towards me.

Under the silver casing, I began to sweat. I couldn't tell if the heat came from the nearing flame or my own body, but inside that suit of hardened powder, it became unbearably hot. I didn't know if I was only imagining it, but I felt pinpricks of pain all over my body, and I wondered if the acid was already beginning to eat away at me the way it had the orange.

I'd always known Hannah hated me, but did she hate me enough to kill me? As the flickering flame approached, I realized I would soon find out if I did nothing. But what could I do? I was trapped in layers of casing acid, unable to move. I had no choice.

I screamed. It was not like a scream you hear in a film, the scream the beautiful woman in the horror movie makes when she sees the monster. It was a horrible, guttural sound that wrenched itself from my throat unbidden. I sounded like a cornered animal, which, I suppose, I was.

Only then did the teacher reappear.

§

The little sores appeared the next day. Places I hadn't noticed the acid beginning to bite into me. A few on my knuckles, my knees, my neck. I looked like I'd been attacked

129

by a swarm of angry but uncoordinated hornets, who left big splotchy marks instead of neat little bites. It made me easy to recognize.

"Oh my god," my cashier at the grocery store had said. "You're the girl from the high school?" She said *the* high school because there was only one in town. And *the* girl because there was only one girl everyone was talking about.

I nodded meekly and continued putting my groceries on the counter. Well, my family's groceries. I was shopping for all of us.

"I am *so* sorry about what those kids did to you," she shook her head and put her hand over her heart, as if just seeing me pained her. While I felt that usual rush of being acknowledged, it was tinged with the fact that she was *really* noticing my scars. Not me, but the fact that I was a victim. "Just a sec. Lemme get my manager." She turned around and shouted, "TED! HEY TED!" A hairy jelly bean of a man bounced over to the counter.

"There a problem Sue?" he asked amiably. Sue gestured to me.

"It's the little acid girl!"

I could feel my face turning bright red. That's not my name, I wanted to say. But I didn't.

"Well I'll be!" He took my hand in his warm, pudgy fingers and looked me in the eyes. "I cannot express my deepest apologies for what happened to you at that school," he said. "Tell you what — round this store, you get your groceries for free!"

"Really?" I managed to murmur. It was the first word I'd said during the whole exchange.

"Of course! We, as a community, gotta be better at takin' care of our kids, don't ya think?"

Before I could come up with a response he said, "Little acid girl, we're gonna treat you right!"

§

As is the way in small towns, news of my newfound fame spread fast. Wanting to jump on the bandwagon, other businesses started making me offers. The beauty salon offered to give me a makeover to hide the scars. The book store told me they heard I was a fan of reading and gave me a gift certificate and a tote bag. The ice cream parlor said I could get a free cone for me and a friend whenever I wanted. I wondered if they knew the cruel irony of the "and a friend" part.

Things were different at school, too. Some students made a big show of being nice to me, saying "Hey! Come sit with me!" or "Why don't I pay for your lunch today?" The problem is, it was more for them than for me. They wanted to see themselves as the hero of my story. But they were the heroes of their own, not mine. My story didn't have a hero. Not even me.

Other students resented me even more than they used to. At first they were just frustrated they couldn't get inside my head. Now I was as unreadable as ever, but also a local

131

celebrity without even trying to be one. It was no wonder that roused some jealousy.

I should have known a reckoning was coming. I was too overwhelmed to read the signs. Hannah was suspended for two weeks, as there was no question that she was the main culprit. The rest of her volleyball cronies eyed me with feline ferocity in the cafeteria, but I was getting so much unwanted attention that I hardly noticed.

It barely even registered with me when Hannah returned to school. Properly chastened by the school's slap on the wrist, she made no more attempts to speak to me. It felt like a small victory. While I still squirmed under the eyes of the rest of the school, at least my usual tormenter was no longer watching me.

But the school didn't take her out of my chemistry class.

Looking back, I was foolish. To think I had won. I didn't have the same mentality as an athlete. I hadn't won at all — the ref had simply given Hannah a red card, and she was waiting out her penalty until she could play another match.

I didn't know there would *be* another match.

Not until one chemistry lab months later, when the teacher forgot to grab enough erlenmeyer flasks for the class and had to make another trip to the storage closet. This time, Hannah said nothing. She simply stood over me, again holding a little plastic canister of casing acid.

Perhaps if I'd known we were still at war, I would have run. I would have called for the teacher, or at the very least done something to protect myself. But I assumed Hannah was long done toying with me, so I simply said, "We're not using that for today's lab."

Unsmiling, Hannah said, "Oh. I know."

§

My parents pulled me out of school. We moved to a big city, where it was easier to be anonymous. Now the kids at school don't ask me why I'm so quiet, which I suppose is nice, but I think it's because they believe they already know the answer. When they think they have me all figured out, I'm not as much of a mystery. The more brazen ones still ask me questions sometimes, though. But they don't ask, "You don't talk much, do ya?"

They ask, "What happened to your eyes?"

I am not a people-watcher anymore. I'm not Little Acid Girl anymore, either; I'm Little Blind Girl. The truth is, I don't really care that Hannah took my old life from me. I only care that she took my identity — and with it she took my name.

Coffee Date with The Eternal One

Originally published in Orion's Beau

She didn't stand out like I thought she would. I thought I would recognize her right away, that some kind of supernatural aura would draw me to her, but when I entered the coffee shop, little bell on the door jingling as I entered, I swept my eyes over the room. No one *looked* like a monster to me.

I saw some movement out of the corner of my eye, and turned to see her wiggling her fingers at me, giving me a crooked smile. Her lips were bright red, which made her look all the more pale. She stirred her coffee idly, though it looked as though she hadn't even taken a sip. I noticed that it wasn't even steaming any more. How long had she been waiting for me? Walking towards her, I felt my stomach begin to twist, and I was suddenly aware of the rapid pounding of my heart.

I jerked the chair across from her back, the wooden legs screeching against the floor.

"Thank you for meeting me," I said breathlessly, trying and failing to fix my unruly hair. Her hair, afterall, was so pristine. Two cascades of silky black locks. I must look so ugly compared to her, so...imperfect.

"No, thank you," she grinned. "I'm happy to be of service. Doing this...counseling, it lets me feel like I'm helping people. I appreciate your willingness to meet me in person. I find these conversations go better when we can be face to face."

"Thank you, thank you," I repeated, wringing my hands. "I'm really lucky to have found you, honestly. I haven't told many people about my, um...my situation, since I didn't think anyone would believe me, but one of my friends...well, she gave me your number."

She didn't say anything, just smiled sweetly and nodded.

"Should we — um — do you want to order food?" I asked.

She laughed, and it sounded like the tinkle of sleigh bells. "No, I don't think I'll be having anything," she nodded towards her cold, untouched coffee.

"Right. Of course," I stammered. "I don't — I don't actually want anything anyway. I'm not that hungry."

"If you're certain," she said. "So, let's get right to it, then. Tell me, how did the two of you meet?"

"I — um —" I stuttered, "at work. I work at this, um, this art gallery. Well, it's not — not a gallery, really. It's a co-op. Like, you can sell your work there, and in return, you have to work there. It —"

"The details don't matter," she cut me off, not unkindly, but it still made me more frazzled.

"Well," I continued my story, "he was looking at some art. My art. I make these, um, ceramics. Like, you know, pottery. Mugs and bowls. Sculptures, sometimes. I went up to ask him if he needed help with anything or if he had any questions and —" I swallowed. "And he turned around and he was the most beautiful man I had ever seen."

She laughed, and even though I was embarrassed I still felt like the laugh was melting me a little, like butter in a hot saucepan. Everything felt just a little smoother as she spoke, the world felt like it lost its sharp edges when she looked at me.

"I'm sorry," she grinned. "It's just...I've heard that so many times before. It's always the same, isn't it?"

"I — um, I don't know," I admitted. "I guess maybe it is. But he turned and I was so shocked I didn't say anything, and he said, 'Sir, how much is this one?' and he held out one of my own mugs to me and I — it was the green one with the purple swirls — and I, I said 'You can have it for free.' And he said —"

"You don't have to tell me everything, you realized," she said, placing her hand on mine. Her voice was like warm honey, but her hand was ice cold. I couldn't help feeling like I wanted her touch, but I drew my hand back reflexively.

"The point is," I rubbed some warmth back into my hand, "he likes the things I make. He said he wouldn't take one for free, but if I made one just for him, then he would take it. So I just, I just sort of started making things for him. And he started showing up to the store every day and every

136

day I would have a new gift for him. It was like...the only thing I ever wanted to do was make things for him. And no one else."

She interlaced her fingers and placed her chin atop the peak of her hands. "And what did you get out of this arrangement?" she asked.

"I mean, I got to see him. That was enough for me."

"It didn't feel...parasitic?" she raised an eyebrow.

"No! No, I mean...you do things for people you love, right?"

"Do you love him?" she asked.

"Yes!" I answered reflexively. "I mean, of course I do. I wouldn't be — there's no doubt in my mind. If there were I wouldn't — I mean, I wouldn't be talking to you. I wouldn't even be considering this. I want to be with him for the rest of my life."

"That's possible, you know, without you making such a drastic choice," she reminded me. She stirred the cold coffee and the spoon clinked on the edges of the mug.

"I know, but...it wouldn't be the same."

"And he loves you, too? Or have your interactions been limited to pottery sales?" Her tone wasn't derisive, but I could tell she still looked at me like a child. Something in her eyes said, *Oh, poor boy, look what you've gotten yourself into.*

"No, I mean we've...we've been together for some time now." Obviously I trusted her opinion; that's why I came to her in the first place. But she couldn't really *know* what it was like. She didn't *know* him.

"How long is some time?" she probed.

"Six months."

"Not that long."

"Long enough to know."

She gave me that lopsided smile. "You'd think that."

We sat in silence for a moment. I waited for her to say something, anything, but she just watched me, and the more she watched me, the more twitchy I felt, so I finally asked her, "So what do you think?"

She sighed, crossing her arms in front of her. "My answer is the same as it always is: no."

My stomach sank. "No?"

"No."

"But I thought —"

"Let me tell you my story," she cut me off. "I was in love, too. But love is only meant to last as long as humans last. It was meant to die with the people who hold it. And if the person who holds it cannot die...what happens to the love?"

"You don't understand," I snapped without meaning to, growing defensive. "You don't know what we have."

"No, I'm sure I don't. But there is a reason that wedding vows say 'till death do us part.'"

"Because people don't usually have another option!" I protested. "I do! *I do!*"

A few heads turned in our direction, and I noticed I was on my feet. Blushing, I sat back down, chastened by the stares of the other patrons. She only laughed.

"I don't know the ins and outs of your relationship," she admitted, "but you, similarly, do not know what it's like to live without the promise of death."

Her words were hard, cold, and I felt them like a frigid hand pressing against my chest.

"How...old are you?" I asked. I mean, of course I'd assumed she was old, older than she looked — she'd have to be — but...were these ancient eyes staring back at me?

She grinned devilishly.

"It's rude to ask a lady her age," she said, then lifted her hand to summon a waiter and ask for the check.

"So...that's it, then?" I asked.

"Yes. That's it."

I swallowed. "Well...thank you for your time." I stood, shakily, and again the chair screeched against the floor.

"I'll...I'll think about it."

"No you won't," she smiled sadly, going back to stirring her cold coffee. "You made up your mind even before you came to see me."

I looked down at my feet, unable to meet her eyes.

"I guess I did."

"Well then. There's nothing more for me to say."

Without looking back, I made my way towards the door. As the bell jangled a final farewell, I could feel her gaze on me, and I knew that she was right, right about everything.

But I also knew I was going to do it anyway. I couldn't help it. And of all people, she should understand. She couldn't help it either.

If You Believe in Fairies

They say there are fairies in these woods, but all I've been able to find are some cool rocks. When I was a kid, I used to build these little houses on the side of trees. I'd find a little nook in the roots, peel up a sheet of moss from the ground and prop it up on some sticks like a tent. I'd collect acorn caps to be little cups, and I'd make a tiny table out of tree bark.

"Don't let anyone touch it," I'd tell my parents. "It's a house for fairies." But the next day, my brother Jeremy would smash it. Jeremy was the kind of kid who crushed butterflies for fun. I was the kind of kid who collected rocks that I thought might be magical. Even though Jeremy kept stealing them and covering them in peanut butter so he could try and feed them to my dog Nacho.

When I went to the woods armed with my creatures-of-the-fey pamphlet, I didn't find fairies. I found a dead snake, an old shoe, and a hornets nest that I thought was abandoned until I tried poking it with a stick.

"There's still hornets in there," a voice behind me said. I screamed, partially because the voice had startled me and partially because some hornets began to emerge from the nest. I turned on my heels and fled, only to slam directly into a solid wall of flesh. The creature behind me was so thickly built that I bounced right off its round belly and landed on my back in the dirt. Scrambling backwards like a confused spider on the forest floor, I saw the speaker in full.

Its rumpled brown skin and drooping snout reminded me of a tiny-trunked bipedal elephant made out of a brown paper bag. Its snout was flanked by two tusks protruding upwards from its lower lip. Its bulbous belly jiggled as it clomped around on its hooves, and its wispy tail whipped around behind it as it looked down on me.

Too fascinated to be scared, I whipped the pamphlet out of my pocket and started to flip through it, looking for some diagram that would identify the rotund creature that towered over me.

"What are you?" I asked conversationally, as one might ask a question like "Oh, what part of Chicago are you from?"

"What does it look like?" the thing demanded gruffly, waving flabby arms in indignation.

"Um..." I leafed through the pamphlet, looking back and forth hurriedly between pages and creature, but no illustrations seemed to fit.

"A troll?" I ventured, "Maybe?"

The creature scoffed so hard its little trunk billowed. "A troll! Oh, that's real nice. Kid wanders into *my* woods and calls *me* a troll."

"I'm sorry!" I stammered. "I just — you don't look like any of the pictures —"

"I," the creature placed a hooved hand on its chest proudly, "am a fairy."

"Oh," I cocked my head to the side, pulling myself off the ground as I brushed off the dirt. The creature didn't look anything like the fairy in the pamphlet — a slender blonde boy with wings like a dragonfly, clad in a tunic made of a maple leaf and strewn with wildflowers. If anything, this creature looked like an indignant humanoid pachyderm with far too many teeth.

All I could think to say was, "I didn't know fairies had tails. Or tusks. Or snouts."

"It's not a *snout*," the creature corrected superciliously. "It's an elongated nostril. If you'll *notice,* there's only one hole at the end, not two."

I didn't want to get too close to the viscous liquid that was dripping out of its end, so I simply took the fairy's word for it. I glanced at the pamphlet to refresh my memory as to what to do upon meeting a fairy. "Offer treasures." Right.

"I don't have any treasure to offer," I admitted. "Well, actually, no, I do. I picked up some cool rocks. Would you like to see them?" I pulled them out of my pockets and held them out like an offering.

"No I would not." The creature put its hooved hands on its hips.

"Okay, but you're missing out."

"What makes you think I'd want that garbage?"

"Well, the pamphlet said —"

The creature snorted again, and this time its elongated nostril danced so dramatically it almost flew over its head.

"Let me see that," it said as it ripped the paper from my hands. "This is ridiculous!" it roared with a grimace. "What kind of body standards are they trying to hold me to? Whoever drew this damn thing has never seen a fairy in their life."

"Well, maybe I can redraw it!" I suggested. "I'll sketch you!"

I attempted a hurried sketch on the back of the pamphlet, but it looked like a rejected Pokémon.

"Just forget about it!" the creature bemoaned when I showed it the final product, crossing its leathery arms. "It's probably for the best," it admitted, once its frustration was quelled. "It's not worth it to try and show people what I really look like."

"Why not?" I asked, starting to pocket my drawing.

"Reality," the creature sighed, "is just too disappointing."

"Well, I didn't find you disappointing," I said.

The fairy fixed me with a skeptical look.

"Really?" it asked, and then a touch more hesitant, "You're not just saying that?"

"Why would I be disappointed?" I asked. "Not only did I meet a fairy, but I found one with a tail *and* tusks *and* an elongated nostril. And I'm really bad at finding things. Like I can't even find my keys most days so I just climb in and out of my window. So this is a *great* day for me."

The fairy's expression softened, and then it broke into a wide, toothy smile, its long nose waggling triumphantly.

"I guess you *did* find some nice rocks, too."

I smiled.

"Yeah, the rocks are nice too."

Dev Fielding and the Call of the In Between

She took my life away Friday night, which was not the ideal start to my weekend.

I never ever expected anyone would want my life that badly.

You see, I think people on the whole are afraid of lawyers. They believe we have the arcane ability to make words dance, to twist what they say into the right shape to suit our dread purpose, to trap them in a labyrinth of contracts and fees. They see us as dangerous, slippery creatures because we make the line between truth and lie blur, and that makes us a threat. Which is ironic, because our duty is to *protect* you from just that happening. The police are the ones who are going to use your own words against you. The corporation that you work for is going to find some way to massage the truth until that "accident" you were involved in becomes your fault. We're the ones trying to help you, not hurt you.

I'm a public defender. I'm not saying that all lawyers honor that duty faithfully, but you'd be hard pressed to find a public defender that isn't doing their work out of a sense of altruism. It's not the most glamorous kind of law practice.

I don't believe that my current client is a good person. In fact, I don't believe she's a person at all. But I believe she is still worthy of a defense just like anyone else, because I know that there is no worse sensation in the world than having no one to stand by you.

This whole business began — or, I suppose I should say, my *involvement* began — when she strutted into my office just before the workday was about to end. From the moment she burst in, I knew something was amiss. You see, my clients do not choose me any more than I choose them. They do not have the means to hire a lawyer themselves, so the government steps in to lend a hand. Or at the very least lend a finger.

People don't generally walk into my office without an appointment, especially not strangers, and *especially* not strangers this finely dressed. I don't mean to stereotype my clients, but *none* of them walk in here in ballgowns. This woman oozed wealth like a particularly pompous slug. But that was where her resemblance to a slug ended. Her sickly slender form put me in mind of a skeleton, and her tight green dress added to the illusion that she was inhumanly skinny. The sight of her was...unnerving. The way she wouldn't stop smiling put me in mind of the Cheshire Cat, like she could disappear in an instant and that smile would still hang in the air. Her eyes shimmered with what I can only describe as menace.

I figured she must be lost, though I can't imagine getting so lost you find yourself in a public defender's office. It's not the kind of place many people find themselves in by mistake.

"Can I help you, ma'am?" I asked. She grinned, and my feeling of unease deepened.

"Yes," she purred. "You can, and you will. You see, you're my new lawyer."

I raised an eyebrow. Had this woman been assigned to me, I would have known. Besides, she didn't seem like the kind of person to go through the proper channels. Rich people tend to think they're too good for those. Then again, rich people definitely tend to think they're too good for public defenders, so I still wasn't sure what she was doing in my office.

"I think you must be mistaken," I told her coolly, lacing my fingers together as I glanced at her criss-crossing silver necklaces. Something about them made me think of spider webs. "My services are reserved for the underserved."

Most people think I deal with all sorts of "unsavories." They have their stereotypes about what kind of person ends up with a public defender. Truth is, most of the people I represent are very pleasant. A lot of them can't afford another lawyer through no fault of their own, simply because they lost their job or they had to pay medical bills or they were homeless. I make a point of being kind to my clients, and they are just as kind to me. This woman was not my client, so I felt no obligation to be kind to her. And if there's one thing I hate, it's people who are entitled.

She laughed that kind of laugh that's grating on the ears, the kind that says, "I know more than you." She sat down even though she hadn't been invited to.

"I don't make mistakes," she informed me. "I've been through a lot of lawyers, you see, so I know how to find a good one. Don't usually find them in places like this, though," she glanced around the office with a hint of disgust in her voice. Truth be told, my office is not luxurious and I am aware of that. I know there are roaches. I know it smells like mold and old paper. I don't mind these things. It's the price, I often tell myself, for justice. It's what I mutter under my breath every time I find mouse droppings on my case files.

"You're wasting your talents here," she continued. "You could be making triple what you make now working for a pharmaceutical company."

"I don't doubt it." Of course the thought had crossed my mind countless times, but I wasn't about to sacrifice my principles to make a little extra money. Or a lot of extra money. It doesn't matter. I was never going to become a corporate lawyer and I knew that the day I decided to study law. "But a good defense should not be a privilege that only the rich can afford. It should be a right."

She laughed again, and this time I felt a sharp pang of indignation. I don't think I am someone who takes myself too seriously. But I am someone who takes their beliefs very seriously, and I didn't take this derision kindly. What exactly was it about justice that this woman found risible?

"Well, I'm sure your precious clients can wait while you're working for me."

"Ma'am, I'm not *working* for you," I told her firmly.

149

"Unless you qualify for my assistance, which I can assure you that you don't, I'm not working for you."

Her smile remained on her face as she examined her dark green, manicured fingernails.

"A lot of my previous ones said that," she mused, speaking of them as though they were particularly wayward pets, "but they all came around."

"Well, I won't be 'coming around.'"

I stood up and started to make a point of packing up my things. Technically I was supposed to stay at work for another twenty minutes, but after all the late nights I've worked I figured I deserved one early exit for the purpose of shooing this woman out. She simply smiled her unnerving smile and said, "You don't have a choice. When I lose a lawyer, I choose a new one. And I choose *you*."

I bit down on a snarky remark about how defense lawyers are not Pokémon, and they are not for you to capture and collect. The only thing that gave me pause was to wonder why such a wealthy person would seek out a lawyer who was, to put it bluntly, cheap. Couldn't she afford anyone? What was it about me that she wanted so badly? The mystery of it all compelled me more than I'd like to admit.

"What...happened to your last lawyer?" I asked before I could curb my curiosity.

"He died," she shrugged, as if she were only saying he had moved away. She met my eyes. "It's dangerous work, you know."

The comment stopped me as I was closing my laptop.

"No, I don't know," I responded. "It's never seemed very dangerous to me."

"Oh, not being a *lawyer*" she clarified. "Being *my* lawyer." I slid my laptop into its case and shoved it into my messenger bag, eager to extract myself from the conversation.

"Good evening, ma'am," I said, though I'm sure she could detect that no part of me wished her a good evening, "and I hope you'll be able to find a lawyer better suited to your needs."

She didn't respond. She just watched me as I made my way out.

"I'll need to lock the door," I told her, the implication being, *get the hell out of my office.*

"Then lock it," she said.

"I can't leave you alone here. There's confidential information —"

"If you're asking me to leave, just ask me to leave."

"Fine," I spat. "Please leave."

Wordlessly, she stood, and when she brushed past me I smelled her. I expected she'd smell like one of those expensive perfumes, like rose and citrus. Instead the scent that wafted off her was that of dirt and rain. Flowers rotting in the mud. Not unpleasant, actually, but not the kind of smell you expect to find on a person, unless they've been digging ditches in a thunderstorm, which this woman didn't seem like she'd been doing at all.

"See you tonight, Mx. Fielding," she said without turning around as she disappeared down the hall. I'm not sure which was more unsettling: her promise to see me later that evening, or hearing her say my name. I'd never given it to her, and hearing it in her voice made me feel as though she'd stolen it and claimed it as her own. Only then did I realize I didn't know *her* name, and for some indiscernible reason that gave me a sense of unease. As though she had a piece of me that I hadn't intended for her to take.

My only plans that night were to go out for drinks with some of my old friends, just like I do every Friday. I couldn't imagine my mystery "client" managing to snake her way into those plans, but her warning — and it *did* feel like a warning — kept me on edge. That evening I told my friends about the obnoxious rich woman who walked into my office that day demanding I represent her.

"Rich people are the worst!" Steve exclaimed, who was always saying things like this because he was self-conscious of the fact that he was making more money than the rest of us combined at his programming job. For people of our generation, it is not "cool" to be wealthy. It's traitorous. It's "cool" to mutter things like "elitist scum" into your beer, which is what Lucy was doing. Reg, who's never been the brightest of the group, looked at me with a furrowed brow, his head cocked to the side.

"Well, are you gonna do it?" he asked.

I stared at him for a moment.

"Of course they're not," Lucy answered for me. "They only take cases from the government or whatever. And besides, it's not like they would *want* to represent her. Right, Dev?"

I nodded, decidedly not telling them about how the woman insisted that I'd be working for her whether I wanted to or not. Even though I hadn't wanted to let her get to me, I did a quick sweep of the bar when I arrived to see if she would, in fact, be seeing me tonight. When I didn't see her around, I relaxed a little. Enough that I was comfortable recounting the whole bizarre tale without being overheard. But if my friends understood how much the whole event disturbed me, they didn't show it. They just laughed. Lucy started talking about the strange orders she had received that week — she's a waitress and someone didn't believe her that a "virgin screwdriver" was just orange juice — and the whole thing was forgotten. By *them*. I was still thinking about it, even when Steve started telling us about the new retail site they have him working on and then quickly backpedaled to explain that he wouldn't actually be making that much more money, even when we had our weekly fight with Reg about whether or not he was too drunk to drive home.

I didn't forget it until I was safely in my own home, door locked, television on, wine in hand. I didn't even bother to change out of my work clothes. I'm thankful for that now, but at the time I was just too tired.

I don't even remember what show I put on. That's how quickly I fell asleep.

And I dreamed.

That part is important, because that's how I knew that what happened next was *not* a dream. I dreamt that I was walking on a street I didn't recognize, but that somehow still felt like home. I was looking out across a canal, lined with brightly colored façades so perfect they looked like little dollhouses. As I walked I watched the rowboats on the water, each holding only one person and a robed gondolier paddling like a little wind-up toy. It was like an ethereal Venice, something about it just uncanny enough to feel like it was nefarious, but nothing obvious that I could point to and say, "Now that's not right." Perhaps it was the fact that the gondoliers were shrouded, their faces, if they had any, obscured by shadow. Perhaps it was the way that the buildings seemed to curve inward, as though the world itself had learned physics through a fisheye lens, making the whole place look like a grotesque cartoon. Or maybe it was the fact that the gondolas were not paddling down the canal, but across it.

Opposite the canal was a towering marble building, with columns reaching up to a triangular pediment. The thing stretched so far into the sky that it looked like it grew thinner at the top. I unquestioningly tread the marble steps and threw open the front doors. Then I woke up.

You know that feeling when you're in the middle of a dream and you're jolted awake, and suddenly you remember who you are? It wasn't like that. Instead my dream melted away to reveal an identical reality. I was still in that marble building, its red carpet stretched out before me. But now I was *really* there.

And I'm sure I don't have to tell you who *else* was there, waiting to greet me.

"No!" I shouted, and whirled around to run for the door, but she caught my arm and turned me back around.

"I'm so excited for you to join my team, Mx. Fielding," she cooed. "Let me show you to your new office."

"I don't *have* a new office!" I ripped my arm away, for the first time taking in the room around me. "Where is this?" I demanded. "How did you bring me here?"

The woman smirked, her nose wrinkling. "This is the In Between," she told me, "and you came here on your own."

"No I didn't," I objected.

"Well, I'll admit I gave you a bit of guidance. There's a reason you don't end up in the In Between every time you drift off to sleep."

My mind swirled with more questions than I could put words to, and only one made its way out of my mouth: "In between what?"

"Hm?"

"You called this 'in between.'"

"*The* In Between," she corrected.

"In between *what*?" I repeated.

She fixed me with a coy look. "You haven't figured it out already?" she asked. "You're supposed to be smart, aren't you?"

The truth was, I already had a guess. But it seemed far too outlandish to actually be the truth. I needed to hear her tell me, *assure* me, that I had been drugged or kidnapped or something like that but still very much in the *real world,* because something inside me was already convinced that I was in another realm entirely and I desperately didn't want it to be true. I would rather that she tell me I had been captured by the mob or organ traffickers instead of where I somehow already knew that I was. But I couldn't bring myself to tell her all that, so I simply said. "I have my suspicions. Humor me. What are we standing in between?"

She flashed that irritating, "I-know-more-than-you" smile that I was already beginning to hate so much.

"Life and death, of course. Let me show you to your office."

How would a normal person react to all of this? I'm not sure I could tell you. Perhaps break down crying, or pray to whatever god they believe in that they will be delivered from this semi-purgatory, or maybe convince themself that it was all a dream that they'd wake up from. None of these things were really my brand. Instead I asked, "Will my office have windows?"

The woman frowned.

"That's not usually the first question I get."

"It's my job to ask the important questions, and right now the most important question is whether or not I'll have windows." This was, of course, a lie. The truth was my mind was spinning far too quickly to come up with a more apt question like, "How do I get out of here?" or "Why does purgatory have boats?" So I decided to play it off like I was taking everything in stride, which I definitely was not. You can't let people know when they've beaten you, you see. You have to let them think that you're always one step ahead of them. That's why seeing the woman's clear confusion brought me a hint of satisfaction, even though she'd just told me I might be dead. Sort of dead. That was another question I hadn't gotten to yet.

She whirled around, her emerald gown whipping around her. "Follow me."

She led me down a red-carpeted corridor, lined with those wooden doors that have frosted glass windows. We must have passed by hundreds of doors, each with a different name across the front. After a good ten minutes of walking it occurred to me to wonder just how many offices there were in this building, and how long this hallway could possibly lead.

"So which do you represent?" I finally asked once I had enough presence of mind to ask a semi-intelligent question.

"How do you mean?" she asked without breaking her stride.

"If this is the place in between life and death, you must be from one of the two. So? Which is it?"

157

She didn't turn around to face me, but I could tell she was grinning fiendishly.

"You're the one with the fancy degree. You tell me."

I thought of the boats. All going against the current, in one direction. Towards us. All going to the same place. My mouth went dry, but I didn't want to show her that I was beginning to feel afraid.

"I have a follow up question, then," I said. "Why does death need a lawyer?"

The woman stopped at a door that had my name emblazoned on it, turning around to face me. "For some, death is easy. Others need a bit of convincing." She turned the knob and pushed the door open.

"Welcome."

I didn't want to give the woman the satisfaction of knowing that I was actually impressed, but I think she heard me gasp a little when I entered the room. The wooden floors gleamed with polish, and the walls were lined with tasteful bronze filing cabinets. At the center was a mahogany desk far nicer than any I'd had in my time of public service, and standing on it was a stained glass lamp. Far more impressive than any of the furnishings were the windows. The whole back wall was glass, looking out onto the canal that I now knew to be something like the River Styx, the gondoliers ferrying departed souls from one side to the other. I pressed my fingers to the glass, mesmerized by the shimmering waters down below. Despite its grim purpose, it was still beautiful. Up close I could see that the desk had been carved with patterns of lilies, and it looked more like it belonged in a museum than in an office. My fingers glided along the smooth finish when I noticed what was sitting on it desk.

"Typewriter?" I asked.

"For your notes."

"You don't have computers here?"

"You won't be needing one. All the pertinent information will be given to you via files." She tapped a little gold hatch mounted on the wall, the mouth of some sort of chute, before walking back over to the doorway.

I bristled at the confidence in her voice. I wasn't *actually* going to work for her. She did know that, didn't she? If she really *was* who she said she was, some kind of agent of death, there should be a choice, shouldn't there? Like making a deal with the devil? Then again, if the devil wanted to make a deal with someone, I imagine it wouldn't be a lawyer, who would surely pore over the contract with a magnifying glass. There's a reason in those stories it's usually old woodcutters or some such who are taken in by the devil. Lawyers are not fooled easily. They also don't make friends easily. It's the price we have to pay. So instead of panicking like my body was desperately begging me to do, I was biding my time, waiting to figure out how I could escape being roped into this whole thing. I'd helped hundreds of people find loopholes in contracts. I didn't care that this woman was some kind of emissary of death. This would be no different.

"Do I get a place to sleep?" I asked, hoping to catch her off guard.

"You won't be needing that either."

"A bedroom?"

"No. Sleep. You're still sleeping right now."

"What —"

"You're spilling red wine all over your nice cream carpet."

"Shit! Not the carpet!" I think that was the first time I let her see me genuinely alarmed. I can keep my composure being told that I've been abducted to be death's lawyer, sure, but I'd just had that carpet put in. I'm very particular about those sorts of things.

She laughed. "The material realm is no longer important, you understand. All that matters now is your work here."

My original plan to play it cool, let her think I'm just going along with everything, and then make a break for it, met a serious roadblock if I was trapped inside my own head. Where was there to run?

"Alright, how do I get out of here?" I crossed my arms, staring her down across the desk.

"And here I was, thinking that you were just getting settled in!" she pouted, leaning against the doorframe. I kept my demeanor cold. It's a learned skill.

"You're not going to just uproot me from my life and expect me to work for you that easily."

"Of course I am," she protested. "I've done it thousands of times."

"Wha —"

"Whose offices did you think we were passing on our way here?" she gestured down the hall. "I've had plenty of lawyers. And they all came here very much in the same way that you did."

"You kidnapped them?" I asked.

She frowned. "I *guided* them."

"Alright, well they must have gotten out somehow. Otherwise, you wouldn't need me. How?" As I asked the question I felt my stomach sink, as I feared I already knew the answer. I was working for *death,* after all. I could hardly expect that my predecessors had all simply retired and fled to Florida. But instead of giving the grim answer I expected, she shrugged.

"It varies," she glanced down the long passage of doorways that we'd traversed, a hint of nostalgia in her voice. "Some served their term. Others quit."

"Alright. What's the term?" Judging by the number of doors we'd passed by on our way here, this woman went through lawyers like a dog goes through chew toys. Perhaps she'd only want me to work one case, then I'd be free.

"One hundred years," she told me, "and a day."

"What?" I gaped. "I won't live that long, let alone be able to work for you!"

"Your immortal soul doesn't age, silly," she twirled her black hair. I prickled at being called "silly."

"And what about my *mortal* body?" I fumed.. "It's just going to sleep for a hundred years?"

"Time works differently here. Hardly a day will pass in the material realm over our next century. The sun may not even be halfway through the sky."

"Well then I quit!" I shouted. "You said that was the other option, right? To quit? Well, I quit."

"I'm not sure you want to do that. You see, there's only two ways out of here. Back across the river," she pointed to the shimmering stream of gondolas, "or through the gate on the other side. And I'm not sure you're ready to go through the gate yet."

Either I'm here for a hundred years, or I die. There was no contract, and there was no way to argue. I was wrong. And I hated being wrong.

"A surprising number of people do eventually quit, but not on the first day," she explained. "Some lawyers come up with such convincing arguments that they convince themselves. Others simply can't take it anymore. One guy made it the whole hundred years, but on one of the last days of his hundred year term, he had to argue the case to his own mother. That sent him over the edge. Said he would rather die right now than convince his own mother to die. Didn't matter much in the end. I got a new lawyer and she convinced her." The cool indifference with which she told this story made me nauseous.

"Most crack under the pressure. Others simply can't see their way back into the human world after spending the majority of their existence here."

At this point I wasn't listening. I was just staring blankly at the shiny wooden desk, thinking about how I would either die, or be staring at the knots in that wood for the next hundred years.

"I'll leave you to get adjusted, then," the woman said, making a move to leave. My voice stopped her.

"I suppose your name is some kind of demon incantation, and if you tell me your real name then my mind will burst into flames," I guessed, only half joking.

She stared at me blankly, looking somehow less ghoulish and more human than she did the first time she'd appeared to me. "No," she finally said. "You just never asked."

"Oh," I blushed, which is not something I did often. "Well, what can I call you, then?"

"You may call me," she turned to look over her shoulder as she closed the door behind her, "Narissa."

§

Narissa told me to spend my time preparing for my first trial, but I've never exactly been the type to do what I'm told unquestioningly. I've had to defend too many people who did exactly what was expected of them, and that's how they ended up in some kind of nasty situation. They didn't read the fine print. Not that there was any fine print for me to read. This was just my job now. That being said, I had no fear of being fired, or even penalized, so I took my time preparing for the case and instead spent my time trying to learn as much as I could about the "In Between." I started by observing Narissa.

Narissa didn't just represent death. She *was* death. I would see her paddling across the river to go back to the living realm, gently touching souls and guiding them here. It was only me and her in the building. For all the robed gondoliers I saw paddling back and forth across the canal, I never once saw one set foot in the building, or even leave its boat. Narissa and I had a whole temple all to ourselves, and the knowledge that there was no one in the building except me and death herself amplified my loneliness tenfold.

Considering the number of souls I saw crossing the river, I couldn't believe that only a day was passing in the outside world. Some days whole multitudes crossed. Others, no one did.

And there *were* days in the In Between. No night, but somehow I just knew when a day had passed and melted into the next one.

Most of my time during the first few days was spent at the towering wrought-iron gate behind the building, affixed to two stone pillars, the bars shaped like climbing lilies. I'd never seen it open, but according to Narissa, that was where the dead souls went if they did decide to move on.

"So, it's heaven?" I ventured. Narissa laughed, an ugly sound coming from her.

"Humans have all sorts of silly ideas about what comes after death, but don't you think it's awfully pompous of them to assume that they're correct?"

I shrugged, prickling a little bit at her mockery as I put my hands in my suit pockets. "Everyone has a different idea of what heaven might be. Just because I call it heaven doesn't mean that I'm referring specifically to the Christian conception —"

"Ah, yeah," Narissa waved a dismissive hand. "A rose by any other name, right? Well then, call it what you will. Heaven. Hell. Elysium. Hades. The Afterlife. There's no name for it. It's simply What Comes After."

I told her I didn't much care for What Comes After and I headed back to my office, but the truth was I was far more interested than I let on. Who wouldn't be? There I was, staring down the greatest mystery of human existence: life after death. I could look straight through the twisting iron bars, but still the realm beyond was a mystery to me. It became a bit of an addiction. When I was certain Narissa wasn't watching me — she often was, though I'm not entirely sure why — I would sneak away behind the building and stare at that gate for hours on end. Something about it was...pleasing. Satisfying, almost. Even though I didn't know what was behind it, just being close to it made me feel like...like I was almost home.

As tempted as I was to spend all days in the In Between staring up at those iron bars, I had to pull myself away every time. I have an inquiring sort of mind and I need some kind of intellectual stimulation to keep me occupied, so I applied myself to work shortly after I arrived, even if the work itself was a bit unsettling. A case file had appeared from the chute on my first day, and curiosity propelled me to read it almost immediately.

My first case was a woman named Cooper Swain. I skimmed through the biographical information — born in Omaha, moved to New York at eighteen, married and divorced twice, etc. — and focused on the important part: she'd tried to kill herself. She'd been pursuing a career in acting her whole life, but she had just been refused the role of her choice one too many times. She auditioned for the part of Lady Macbeth and when she found out that she'd been passed over for the role, she gave up. She dressed herself up in her most ostentatious gown, painted on a full face of makeup, bought flowers that she strewn around her apartment and tied into her hair, and drank a full bottle of wine. Then she swallowed as many sleeping pills as she could before she lost consciousness.

I know I may come across as a cold person. I've been told many times that on the first meeting I seem aloof, reserved, even judgmental. But I am not a monster. Contrary to popular belief, I do have empathy — I have a lot of it. Otherwise I wouldn't have taken on a career that requires so much. So reading Ms. Swain's story, I did not relish the idea of trying to convince her to stay dead. It seemed counter to all the principles I stood for. Wasn't the core of my belief system that everyone is worthy of life? Isn't that why I represent the underrepresented? The sheer cognitive dissonance of it all was almost enough to make me want to go to Narissa and tell her that I was ready to end it all now. How would she react if I didn't even try? Would she just "fire" me now and be done with it?

And yet, I somehow knew that throwing the trial was not an option. I was not defending Cooper Swain. I was defending Narissa, and the virtues of death. And everyone deserves a defense. I believe I even said that aloud to myself a few times to remind myself why I was even going through with this. It was not an easy thing to do, but I prepared myself for the trial just like I would any other.

§

"There's someone I'd like you to meet," Narissa announced as she sat herself down on my desk one day. I scowled, not pleased to have the sacred space of my office invaded, but that only seemed to satisfy her.

"I'm busy," I told her, looking back down at my work. She pulled the pen from my hands.

"But you work for me," she said, tapping the purloined pen against her temple, "so I get to tell you when you're busy and when you're not. And right now," she stood, gesturing for me to follow her to the door, "you are completely free."

I sighed and followed her into the grand red-carpeted foyer where I'd first entered the building. Standing there was a woman — the first person I'd seen in the building other than Narissa. I stopped in my tracks upon seeing her, and while it was not the most dignified thing in the world, I think my mouth hung open.

She was beautiful. Now, I need you to understand something about when I say beautiful: we are *taught* what it means for a person to be beautiful. One day we are told it means a slim waist and the next day it means round thighs. When we describe people as "beautiful," we mean they adhere to the image that we have been told is "beauty." When I say that the woman I saw was beautiful, that is not what I mean. I don't mean anything about her features was particularly aesthetically pleasing. She could have chosen any form she pleased, and I am certain I still would have called her beautiful. She was beautiful in the same way that a flower is beautiful. Naturally. She was a collection of colors and shapes and textures that came together in harmony to form one beautiful being. She was radiant like I imagined an angel would be, but what she radiated was not light. It was...energy.

The form she chose to take when she appeared to me was that of a chubby black woman clad in a loose purple gown that billowed behind her when she moved. Atop her mass of black curls was a crown of daisies.

"She always wears that stupid thing," Narissa muttered. I could have sworn I heard jealousy creeping into her voice.

"It's a pleasure to meet you," I said, stepping forward, my hand extended. "My name is Dev Fielding."

"Oh, I know," said the woman, smiling as she gripped my hand. "I always keep track of the creatures *that* one brings in." I recoiled a bit at being called a creature, but I suppose to her, I was one. Like an ant, perhaps. A worker and not much more.

"This is Freya," Narissa introduced from behind me, "and she's —"

"Your counterpart," I interpreted. Freya raised her eyebrows in astonishment.

"Well, it's not that hard to figure out," I explained. "The only other person I've ever seen in this building is Narissa, and look at her —" I gestured to her gaunt frame and pale face, and was met with a menacing glare. "Everything about her says *death*. Then you come in here, and you look like this —" I gestured to Freya's vibrant dress, her wild curls, and her crown of daisies. "It's not difficult to guess who you might be."

Freya spoke right past me. "You've got yourself a good one this time," she told Narissa, and again I bristled at being treated like an accessory.

"May I call you Freya?" I asked in hopes to win her attention back. She nodded, and her curls bobbed with her head.

169

"Well, Freya, I presume I'll be seeing you in the courtroom for my first trial?"

"Of course!"

I adjusted my glasses. "Well, I'm looking forward to it. Now, if you don't mind, I have more preparation to do for the aforementioned trial, and I'll be needing to get back to it."

I whirled around and headed back towards my office, barely registering the surprise on Narissa's face.

"Did you just..." Freya began, "Did you just turn your back on me?" There was no malice in her voice, just genuine shock. Only once she asked the question did I realize how curt I must have seemed to her. Here she was, the personification of life itself, radiating vivacity, and I had just said I was more interested in my paperwork. Perhaps that was a stupid thing to do, but I've always said that if there is a God, I'd never bow to him; I'd simply ask him what he thinks makes him so special. And now that I was there, faced with actual deities, I'd done almost exactly that. I'd simply run out of patience with them.

I shrugged, turning partially back around to meet her eyes. "I don't mean to be rude, Freya," I explained, "but I know who I work for, and it isn't you." As I made my way down the hallway, I heard her coo, "Oh, you've got a sharp one this time, Narissa! This one will keep me on my toes."

I'd be lying if I said I didn't give a little grin, but thankfully no one could see.

§

The trial came unannounced. I figured Narissa would give me some warning, but no. She simply appeared in my office one day and said: "Come. It's time."

I followed her down a long corridor. Unlike the hall where my office was, this hall had no doors at all. It was just a seemingly endless line of walls and red carpet.

"What will it be like?"

"Not much different from a normal courtroom."

When she parted the towering wooden doors in front of me and ushered me into the room, I realized Narissa had probably never set foot in a normal courtroom. The hall I was shepherded into looked nothing like it. There was no bench, to begin with. Instead there was a marble throne, and seated upon it was a woman I recognized to be Cooper Swain. She wore no robe and held no gavel. Instead, she sat up straight with her legs crossed, her eyes darting around the room anxiously. To her right was Freya, lounging in a cushy purple armchair. The matching green one to the left of the throne I could only assume was reserved for Narissa. No desk marked my post. Where the defense should have been, there was only a single stool. And where the prosecution should have been, there was nothing at all.

"Where's her lawyer?" I asked. Narissa laughed.

"She's *life!*" she exclaimed. "She doesn't need one."

"That's hardly fair," I grumbled. Narissa raised an eyebrow.

"Haven't you heard? Life isn't fair."

Before I could respond she sauntered off to her green armchair.

Cooper Swain wore that gown that I'd read about, the one that she'd chosen to die in, and I saw that it was stained with red wine. Her face was still made up, but there were mascara tear streaks running down her face.

I took my post on the stool, alone, waiting for the trial to begin. If I was supposed to be the one who started things off, no one had told me that, so I wasn't going to go around trying to guess at what it was they wanted me to do. I'd already done enough work for them. But no, I didn't need to do anything, it turned out. Ms. Swain looked down at Freya, who nodded and said, "Whenever you're ready, love."

The dead woman glanced over to me. I met her gaze and gave her a warm smile. Like I said, I have a bit of a reputation for being unfriendly, but convincing scared people to trust me is also a crucial part of my job. When I'm trying to be, I believe I can be very approachable. It seemed to work, as Ms. Swain's body relaxed when I nodded to her encouragingly.

"Hi," she started, standing up. "My name is Cooper, and, um..." she wrung her hands, looking down. "I wanted to die. I tried to die. But now...now I don't know what I want." She looked as though she were going to say more, but she just glanced at me and sat back down again. As of cue, Freya stood.

"Ms. Swain —" she began.

"Please call me Cooper," the dead woman requested meekly.

"Of course, darling," Freya said. "Cooper. Here is my opening statement." I expected Freya to launch into a speech about the virtues of life, about the joy of living, about all the wonderful things that Cooper would lose if she crossed over to What Comes After. But she didn't do that. Instead, she said: "Tell me about your mother."

It wasn't as though I could object — who was there to object to? But even if I could, I was too dumbstruck to say anything. How was that an opening statement? Cooper didn't seem to notice.

"My mother is the kindest person I know," she knit her fingers together and looked down at them. "When we were growing up, we didn't have that much, but she always — she worked really hard for us. She never wanted me to feel like I had to give up on my dreams because I needed to make money." She looked away, and her eyes began to fill with tears. "Maybe I've failed her. I don't know. She worked so many jobs and I can't even seem to find one."

Freya approached the bench and reached up to give Cooper a comforting tap on the knee. "You haven't failed her," she murmured, and her voice was like warm cream, thick and rich. "She is so proud of you for following your dreams. In fact, she's thinking of you right now."

Cooper's eyes lit up. "She is?" she asked.

Freya nodded. "She's wondering what you must be up to tonight."

Cooper buried her face in the heels of her hands and sobbed. Freya turned to me grinning, gave me a little curtsey, and murmured, "Your turn."

I looked up at the bawling woman up on the throne, uncertain if I could bring myself to convince her to die. She already looked so broken. Wouldn't I only break her further? But I was not defending her. I was defending Narissa. And if I refused to do it — well, then I would die. And if I did poorly...well, Narissa hadn't actually warned me about that. Either way, I couldn't die yet. I still had clients to represent at home, after all. If I died, they'd be stuck with another lawyer that, if I'm being honest, simply wouldn't compare to me. I adjusted my glasses and stepped forward.

"Cooper," I said, and she lifted her face from her hands, her cheeks now completely smeared with running makeup. "You're an actress. A performer. Isn't that right?"

She wrung her hands. "Not a very good one," she murmured.

"You and I both know that's not true," I chided her gently. "Your performance in *Who's Afraid of Virginia Woolf* last year was phenomenal."

Cooper's face brightened. "You...you heard about that?" A proud little grin found its way onto her face.

"Of course I did! Cooper, I've heard about all your acting successes. You've led a wonderful career. It just so happens that after you moved to the big city —"

"I'm not good enough for New York," she cut me off, and I could see that she was already preparing to sob again.

"Now that's not true," I countered, "because you know that you're a talented actress. You know that you earned that standing ovation at the end of *A Streetcar Named Desire*. It just so happens that the city hasn't yet recognized your brilliance. But isn't this," I indicated her gown, "your most brilliant performance yet?"

She sniffled, pondering this.

"Won't that casting director regret his choice? The talent he wasted? You *could* choose to wake up," I gave her a knowing smile, "but where's the drama in that?"

If someone had given me this argument, I would have laughed in their face. But I had read Cooper Swain's file. I knew all about how she faked a seizure in sixth grade so the other middle school students would finally have a reason to know her name. I knew all about how she pretended to be an alcoholic for years so that her friends would finally host an intervention for her. I knew all about how she made her choice to end her life because then she'd be showing all those "uppity rich actors" what "real Lady Macbeth material looked like." So I wasn't surprised to see her turning over my argument in her head.

Freya was already standing before I'd made it back to my stool, asking Cooper to think of her younger brother. I felt

175

a little flame of rage burning inside me unbidden. Her job was so *easy,* wasn't it? At their core, most people don't want to die. So she hardly had to do anything at all! I suppose that's why Narissa got the advantage of hiring someone out. She just sat in her green armchair, watching, her thin pale lips just slightly curled into a whisper of a smile. Immediately after my moment of anger I felt a pang of guilt. What was I even angry about? That a woman's life would be saved?

I'm not sure how long Freya and I went back and forth for. It could have been a few minutes or it could have been days, but somehow we both knew when it was over. I went back to my stool, and Narissa stood by Freya's side. Cooper rose from the throne and approached them, wiping mascara smears from her face. She looked back and forth between the two women, took a deep breath, and wordlessly took Freya's hand.

"Excellent choice, darling," Freya hummed, and she guided Cooper down the aisle and out of the courtroom.

As the doors slammed shut behind them, Narissa crossed her arms and turned to me.

"You lost," she hissed.

I shrugged. "Is that really any surprise?"

"You were supposed to be a good one."

"I am. But you've given me an impossible task."

She shook her head. "Not impossible."

"You know, I *actually* tried," I told her, "but what if I didn't? What would you do if I just refused to participate?"

She crossed her arms. "What do you think?"

"I imagine you send me through the iron gates."

"No. Only you get to choose to do that."

"So what's keeping me from giving up?"

"You are."

"I don't —"

"Why did you try this time around, hm? If you think this job is so horrible, so 'impossible,' then why did you even try?"

"I — um —"

For the first time I was at a loss for words in front of her. Finally I landed on an answer. "It just seemed like the right thing to do."

"Hm," she snorted with a self-satisfied grin. "I think you'll soon figure out why."

As she stalked away, her heels clicked on the marble floor and she called over her shoulder, "Your heart wasn't in it. Do better!"

§

I didn't do better. At least, not for a very long time. Convincing people to give up on life is neither an easy nor a pleasant task, and often I hated myself for doing it. Each time I felt relieved when I lost, and I think Narissa could tell, because each time she reprimanded me. It wasn't that I was trying to lose. I believe I gave some commendable arguments. Still, the people I argued before were still too attached to their lives to be convinced to part with them. I honestly wasn't sure what I was even doing there.

A man who'd been stabbed in a robbery and was currently bleeding out on the sidewalk. A person who'd fallen off a sailboat and was just seconds away from drowning. A woman who'd fallen from a third-story window and was currently in a coma. Most didn't even give my argument a second thought. When they found out that another chance at life was on the table, they took it.

I didn't win my first case until Santiago Cercas, whose body was currently sinking to the bottom of the Mediterranean Sea after jumping out of a "party plane" off the coast of Ibiza on a dare.

"Now I could stand here and try to convince you that the life you lived was not worth living, but let's face it, you and I both know that would be a lie," I said, consulting the bulleted list of his follies in my notes. He beamed, nodding approvingly.

"The life you led was, honestly, enviable. You've done things most people can only dream of: skydiving. Backpacking across Europe. Getting arrested for public urination. Jumping off a bridge and surviving. Meeting Paul Rudd at a party and, if I remember your file correctly, hooking up with him after. In fact, you had an incredibly impressive sex life. The sheer range of genders is unparalleled."

He leaned back in his chair, smiling smugly, his still wet clothes dripping onto the marble. "Hey, I don't judge, baby."

I forced myself to smile. "The reason I remind you of all this," I continued, "is that you are the kind of person to never say no to an adventure. You stare down a dare and take it on fearlessly. And what is What Comes Next if not the next adventure? What is this trial if not a dare?"

He leaned forward and rubbed his chin contemplatively. Now a genuine smile crept its way onto my face, but I suppressed it, lest I show Freya how satisfied I was with myself.

"Besides," I continued, "wouldn't you rather quit while you're ahead? You're not the kind of person to die as an old man, going quietly in his sleep. No! You want to go out with a bang. With panache!"

I could tell from the look on his face that he didn't know what "panache" was, so I backtracked.

"Isn't this your ideal way to go? Looking incredibly sexy, doing something impressive, surrounded by your friends, completely inebriated? This is your perfect death. Don't waste that."

I could see his eyes light up. He sat up again, a coy smile on his face.

"So lawyer person," he said, "are you saying...that you're *daring* me to die?"

I reeled a bit at the question, surprised that this was the part of the defense he latched onto. However, there is an ancient saying among us lawyers, and it goes like this: whatever works, works.

"I suppose I am," I followed his lead. "I dare you to walk through that gate unafraid. The gate that most people go through unwillingly. You want to be different? You want to be brave? This is the biggest opportunity! You could literally laugh in the face of death."

He looked down at Narissa and started shouting, "Ha! Ha! Ha ha!" Narissa shot me a look but I could tell she was impressed. I didn't even dare to look at Freya, who I knew must be fixing me with the coldest glare she could muster, which, coming from her, was probably lukewarm at worst.

"Hold on just a second," Freya stood abruptly, her dress flouncing around her as she did. "You can't just dare him to die!"

"Oh, can't I?" I asked in wide-eyed innocence, knowing that this would infuriate her even further. I was getting to know her quite well, it turned out, because when I saw her give a tight smile I knew it meant that hot anger simmered just beneath the surface.

"Mr. Cercas," she side-stepped in front of me, "if the thrill is really what you're after, isn't that all the more reason to carry on living? I mean, think of all the things you haven't yet done."

Santiago rubbed his chin in contemplation, leaning back in his chair.

"I dunno, lady," he mused. "I think I've kinda done it all."

"Surely there's something —"

"Liver failure?" I suggested. "Or maybe some form of cancer. Seems like everyone gets cancer these days."

Freya's head snapped in my direction, and she stared at me aghast, shocked that I would dare interrupt her. Again I shrugged with feigned innocence and waved her on.

"Yeah, I don't want any of that shit," Santiago shook his head. "Dying of old age is for posers."

I had no idea what he meant, but I still nodded in affirmation.

"Or," Freya countered, "you could die with the knowledge that you've had a life well lived."

"Nah!" Santiago stood up. "If I wanted to live well I would have eaten vegetables and shit." He turned to look at me with mischief in his eyes.

"But you," he said, "you can keep talking."

"I don't have anything else to say. Either you take the dare," I gave him a meaningful glance, "or not."

He hopped off the chair and sauntered toward me.

"Alright lawyer person. You're on. Take me to the gate." He leaned in closer so that the entities couldn't hear, his eyes flicking up and down over me, "And between you and me, if I were still alive? I would hit that."

"You're not, though," I reminded him, and gestured down the aisle, where Narissa was already by the door, ready to guide him to What Comes Next.

§

"That was so sneaky," Freya fumed. Well, I'm not sure I'd call it fuming, because she was still smiling, and I could tell that she was at least a bit awed. We'd all been there to see him pass on. He gave a salute to Freya, a wink to me, and then took Narissa's hand as she guided him through the stone columns.

I shrugged, hoping to project indifference so she wouldn't glean just how self-satisfied I was, so she continued, "It's not often I get to see someone pass through those gates. For the ones who don't get a trial, she brings them through on her own. And when they do get a trial — well, as you know," she tossed her hair, "I usually win."

"I know," I gave her a little lopsided smile. "But not always."

"Oh ho ho," she laughed, "you're a little bastard."

I shrugged again. "Maybe," I said, and headed back towards my office.

§

It was my first win, and it wasn't my last. Naturally most of my trials were losses — we are hard-wired to want to be alive. It's not easy to counteract that. But if I could find what made that person tick — their unwavering belief in God, a sense of destiny, a life insurance plan that could save their family financially — then I could find a reason they would *want* to stay dead. The more trials I fought, the more

I realized I was only helping people discover what they truly wanted. You see, once you gain some perspective, you realize there isn't anything inherently better about being alive. It's just that most of us prefer it because we *are* alive, and we want to stay that way. It's not because life is somehow inherently superior to death — we're just risk averse. It's a kind of emotional inertia. A body alive wants to stay alive. We tell ourselves, why ruin a good thing? But under certain circumstances, life may not *be* such a good thing.

Each time I won, Freya was both enraged and impressed in equal measure. She masked it well. I don't think it was in her nature to be angry — or, at least, not to *seem* angry. She was a pressure cooker full of hot emotions, but they all simmered under the surface, hidden by a smiling face and a crown of daisies. She was— well, she was *life*. Everything Narissa wasn't. While everything about Narissa was hard and cold, Freya's feelings ran hot, like a broken faucet.

Not to be conceited, but I can see why my defenses made her angry: I was good. I was excellent. Each win meant nothing to me, but for her, it was something being ripped away. She loved each life dearly, and to have one of her precious beings snatched up by Narissa was the greatest pain imaginable for her. And with me on Narissa's side, she was losing much more than she was used to. She was still winning most trials, but even losing a few was more than she was comfortable with.

I suppose that was a bit of a lie — the wins didn't mean *nothing* to me. While I did feel a touch triumphant after each win, it always melted into uncertainty: had I been right? I mean, had I been *right* that death was better? Should *I* be moving along as well? What was there for me in my old life, anyway? The few friends I had weren't particularly close. I had no family to speak of. The thing I really lived for was my work. And I was doing that same exact work in the In Between, so what was the point of going back?

But I'd always have to remind myself: defending Narissa and defending members of the public were not the same task. Narissa could always find a new lawyer — she'd just scoop one up like she had me. Many members of the public don't have that option. If I let myself die sitting on my couch, letting red wine spill onto my carpeting like a rapidly growing blood stain, then my clients would be left without anyone. I know that I may act like they're just that — clients. But I know that for many of them, their whole way of life is on the line. Each time I went out to the gate, I thought of them, and I thought of how if I gave in to that magnetism that was pulling me towards whatever was beyond those stone columns, I would be leaving them. Yes, they'd be assigned to another public defender. But not one like me.

The more trials I won, the more I would stand by that gate.

I got careless. Narissa saw me.

"It's beautiful, isn't it?" she asked.

"Yes," I answered without looking away. "It is."

"Do you hear it?"

"Hear what?"

"The call. Surely you do. Everyone does." Until she pointed it out, I hadn't even noticed. But once I was listening for it, I heard what she meant. It was like a voice singing on the other side of the gate, luring me in like an invisible siren.

"Did you ever stand near a ledge and hear a little part of your brain urging you to fall off?" Narissa asked abruptly.

"I suppose."

"It's normal. Everyone has it. It's your brain trying to get you out of a dangerous situation by taking the quickest way out. Trying to take control. They call it *l'appel du vide*."

"The call of the void," I translated. Narissa smiled.

"You know your French, I see."

I shrugged. "I took a semester in Strasbourg."

"Of course you did," Narissa laughed. "You see, what living people don't know is that it's not *really* the call of the void at all. It's the call of this place. The In Between. It's the call of that gate, right there, begging you to come home. To take control of the situation. To jump off that ledge."

"Funny," I mused, still eyeing the wrought iron curls. "If death were to have a voice, I wouldn't expect it to sound like that."

"How does it sound?"

"Sweet." But that wasn't the word I was looking for. The right word didn't come to me until Narissa had already walked away, and I was standing there alone, listening to the unearthly singing. And in that moment I knew what it was: gentle.

§

It was a rare occasion that Narissa spoke to me on a topic other than business. She'd appear in my office unannounced and say, "Have you read the next file? Challenging one to say the least. You've never been particularly successful with old ladies so I hope you've been taking notes" or "You were too cold last trial. If you're not friendly enough then no one will like you," which was certainly ironic coming from her. Whatever it was she popped in to say, it was always to-the-point. She made it very clear that small talk was not in her vocabulary, which was fine by me because it wasn't something I was particularly fond of either. This made it all the more jarring when she broke her usual veneer of formality to say something...personal.

"Does it hurt?" she once asked. We were walking back from the lily-clad gates after a successful trial — an old recluse that didn't have much going for him in the way of family or friends, so it hadn't exactly been a hard sell. We were climbing the marble steps beneath the columns when she stopped abruptly and turned to look out at the gondolas. I followed her gaze.

"The trials?" I asked. "Of course it hurts. Just because I do my job without complaining —"

She gave a sharp chuckle.

"—just because I do my job," I corrected, "doesn't mean I enjoy it. Convincing people to die feels like...well, honestly it feels like I'm the one killing them. And if that's the case, then I'm a murderer hundreds of times over. Of course that hurts. You probably don't know the meaning of the word guilt, but I carry around more of it than any human was ever supposed to. And that's what hurts. The weight of it."

Once it all came pouring out of me I realized that I must have been waiting for her to ask, to show the slightest bit of interest in how I was handling it. But she didn't respond. She didn't even turn to look at me. She just stared at the gondolas.

"That's not what I meant," she said. "Of course the job hurts. You're not the first lawyer I've had, remember. And they've all said the same thing. That it hurts," a shadow of a grin crossed her face, "like hell. But no, that's not what I meant. I know that already."

"Then what did you mean?"

"Knowing it'll happen to you too."

"Oh."

I too looked out at the gondolas, and imagined myself as a passenger, passively being ferried from one side to the other.

"No," I decided. "I mean, it certainly doesn't feel great, but it doesn't hurt any more than breathing or sleeping or eating. I don't think anything that everyone lives with their entire life can really count as pain."

Narissa said nothing. She only nodded.

"Does it hurt for you?" I surprised even myself by asking. "Knowing that it *won't* happen to you?"

"Yes," Narissa responded without hesitation. And for the first time, I felt a touch of sympathy for her. For the first time I realized there was a well of profound sadness beneath her pale façade, and it was a kind of sadness I would never comprehend. And oddly enough, that was what made Narissa feel more like a person. Isn't that pathetic? That pain is the thing that gave Narissa an ounce of humanity?

"Well, mortality's not all it's cracked up to be," I told her, knowing she didn't want my pity. I don't know what she wanted. Maybe she didn't want anything. Just to have someone to tell. I began ascending the steps again in hopes that she would follow, but she didn't. She still stared out at the canal, so motionless she could have been carved out of marble. It's incredible, really. Freya was always moving. But Narissa could be impossibly still. So I left her there, in a tableau of godly contemplation like a stone angel atop a grave.

§

I saw even less of Freya, but when we did happen to cross paths she never mentioned the trials. I couldn't tell if in her eyes I was truly her enemy, or if it was all a game to her. Oh, I know her anger at me was genuine enough, of that I was sure. The look on her face when I gained too much headway in a trial made it clear that she felt true, honest rage. But so does a child when you beat them at Monopoly. That's not to say that Freya was a child, but that there was something childlike about her. The way she moved, the way she smiled, the way she always seemed like she wanted to play with me even though I could have sworn that moment ago she hated me with a passion.

I'd rarely see her in the temple, but occasionally she'd appear in the red-carpeted hallways. I think perhaps she was visiting Narissa. That was another one of the mysteries I couldn't quite parse out: were the two of them friends? I think perhaps even they didn't know. But I do think they were lonely, so they would pay each other the occasional visit.

"Beautiful day, isn't it Dev?" she'd say as she passed me in the hallway, case files clutched in my arms.

"All days are the same," I'd respond flatly.

"Ah, but it's beautiful now that I'm here."

And you know what? She was right. And she knew that, which is why she laughed when I rolled my eyes in begrudging agreement. She made everything beautiful, and without fail I left her company feeling a little happy and a little scared.

On the whole, I avoided conversation with Freya unless my curiosity became just a little too hungry to ignore.

"Do you get to choose?" I once asked her. She laughed as if this were a joke.

"Choose what, silly?" she asked.

"What you look like. You and Narissa."

She pouted coquettishly. "Do you not like the way I look?"

Of course this was another one of her little jokes. It was impossible *not* to like the way she looked. I frowned at the evasion. "I'm asking —"

"Life is rich," she cut me off, "so I want everything about me to be rich. My skin, my body, my voice — I want to look like life feels."

And truthfully, she did.

§

The trial that broke me started like any other, and I think that's the part that angers me the most. The case I received in the chute was nothing special. The dead man was Noel Carpenter, who had died in a car crash when he swerved to avoid hitting an old lady. I didn't find anything particularly useful in his biographical information — no religious history, no problems he was avoiding, nothing that would make him want to stay dead — so I went into the trial perfectly ready to lose. Narissa walked me down the corridor same as always, but when she threw open the doors, I froze at the top of the aisle.

"Something wrong?" she asked innocently.

At first I said nothing. I stared ahead of me at the marble throne.

"Dev?" she asked again.

"You gave me the wrong case file," I murmured, eyes still fixed on the figure at the other end of the room.

"Oh, I don't send the case files, dear. Freya does that."

"She...she sent me the wrong one?"

"On purpose, I imagine. She doesn't make mistakes. As she reminds me so often," she added with an almost imperceptible eye roll.

"She's not allowed to do that!" I fumed.

"She's allowed to do whatever she wants. Need I remind you that life —"

"Life isn't fair, yes, I remember. Now how the hell am I supposed to — what do I —" At a loss for words, I simply gestured mutely at the throne. Narissa looked between me and the man sitting by Freya.

"Oh," she smiled, placing a pale finger to her pale chin. "You know that man?"

"He's my friend!" I exclaimed. Well, maybe friend was a strong word. But I'd known Reg for years. We'd gone to undergrad together, and while we were never exactly close during those days, I was still seeing him with Lucy and Steve every Friday night when I was in the land of the living. He had become a staple of my life. And hadn't I just seen him? From my perspective, it had been decades since Narissa had spirited me away, but in the real world only a few hours had passed. Had he died the same night I'd gotten drinks with him? How could that happen?

Before I could express any of this to Narissa, before I could put words to my disbelief or to my anger at Freya, he saw me.

"Dev?" he asked in a feeble voice, standing up. "Oh thank God. Dev!" He leapt up off the bench before I could respond and raced towards me, encasing me in his arms. I'm not sure if he and I ever hugged in our lives — I'm not much of a hugger — but in that moment he gripped me like a talisman, squeezing me so tight I almost couldn't breathe. Tentatively I wrapped my arms around him in kind, and I could feel his body shake with sobs.

"I'm so scared," he whispered in my ear. "I don't know what's happening. I don't know what's going on. But — but you're here too, so it's okay. I'm so glad you're here, Dev. Jesus, I'm so scared."

"It's alright," I murmured, gently caressing his shoulder. I've never been much for comforting people, but that seemed the appropriate thing to do. "Everything is fine. There's nothing to be afraid of. Everything is fine."

Over Reg's shoulder I could see Freya, grinning victoriously. It was difficult to be angry at her. She was too bright, too lovable, to find any real fault in. Even though it was a cruel trick, it was hard to see it as anything other than impish. Just a little joke between her and me. Even though anger burned inside of me, I couldn't seem to direct it at her.

Then I understood.

This was not just a sneaky way to get me to throw a trial. This was her attempt to make me quit.

Freya was trying to kill me.

"What a coincidence," she mused, sitting askew in her purple chair, "that you know each other."

"Did you arrange this?" I asked, and I found that it was easier than I had expected to keep the malice out of my voice. Freya shook her head.

"I have no control over who dies, or when. Narissa doesn't either. We're just here to guide them on their way."

Reg looked back and forth between Freya and me. "Am I...dead?" he asked.

"Go sit up on the throne," I directed, and he did as he was told. As I took my post at my stool, Narissa came up behind me.

"So will you do it?" she whispered. I'm not sure I believe her capable of emotions, but I could have sworn I heard an edge of fear creep into her voice. She didn't want to lose me.

"Of course I will," I answered without turning around. "It's my job."

"There are plenty of jobs no one should do."

"But not mine. My job is a job worth doing."

I stepped forward, looking up at my friend.

"Dev," he asked shakily, "what's happening? Am I dead? Why are you here? Are you dead too? Is this...is this all real? Is it in my head?"

I adjusted my glasses. "No, Reg, it's all real. You're not dead. Yet. I'm not dead either. I'm just...dreaming."

"I don't understand."

I laughed despite myself. "I don't either," I admitted. I turned to Narissa. "How did he —" I caught myself. "How did he end up here?"

"Car crash," Narissa glanced down at some files I didn't realize she had been holding. So *she* had received the correct case. I was the only one left in the dark. "He'd been drinking —"

"Yes, I think I remember that," I sighed. I'm not sure how long I'd been in the In Between — time doesn't quite work there in the same way. But it must have been about thirty years since that Friday night I'd spent with my friends. Still I remembered pleading with Reg to let us call him a cab, and him refusing as he often did.

"You were right," he whimpered. "I know, it was stupid...I know that now." His eyes lit up with sudden fear. "Is that why you're here? To punish me? Is this hell?"

Again, I couldn't help but laugh at the fact that my presence made him assume he was in hell.

"No," I assured him, "you're not in hell. You're not in heaven either. Think of this as purgatory. You get to choose if you move on or not."

He furrowed his brow. "So why are you here?"

"I work here."

He stared at me blankly. "You didn't...you never told me that you were a lawyer for hell."

This time we both laughed.

"I was only recently hired."

"So this is not...this is not a dying hallucination or something? You're really you?"

I nodded.

"And what's your job?"

"I'm here to convince you to die."

"Oh."

I swallowed. Freya hadn't given me a chance to prepare a defense, but unfortunately, I didn't need to. I knew Reg. And that meant I knew what to say.

"Back in junior year," I began, "we went to a party together. Do you remember? The baseball team was throwing it, I think."

"Yeah," he smiled fondly, "I do. You were being such a hardass about everything. Like you wouldn't do any of the Jell-O shots because you didn't know who made them so there was 'no accountability' or something."

I grinned sheepishly, pushing my glasses up my nose. "I stand by that," I told him, "but that's not why I bring up that night. Around three in the morning, the party was deserted, and you were puking into the trash can of our dorm's third floor lounge. The rest of our friends had fled, and I stayed with you while you heaved up everything you drank."

His face scrunched up. "I don't remember much of that night, honestly."

"Yes, I imagine. You were blacked out by then, I believe. But you wouldn't stop talking. At first I found it annoying, but then you started to tell me intimate things. Personal things."

I saw his face turn bright crimson.

"You never told me that. How much did I —"

"A lot," I interrupted. "I never told you, no, because I didn't want to embarrass you. I knew that you would — well, I knew you would look exactly as you do now. Mortified. So I decided I would spare you. But now...well, now it's relevant."

"What...what did I tell you?"

I drew in a long breath, and let it out slowly. I did not want to say this. To this day I'm not entirely sure why I did. Perhaps it was the sense of duty that I felt towards Narissa. Perhaps it was pity for Reg. Perhaps it was just blind commitment to my job. But I didn't think I could stop myself from saying what I said next.

"You told me about your sister, Julia. You told me about how you lie awake thinking about her every night. How she died far away from you, without ever getting to say goodbye. How it torments you that you could never see her again, could never tell her all the things you wanted to. How you had just been in a fight, and you would never be able to tell her that you were wrong and stupid. And that you loved her. You would never get to tell her that you loved her ever again."

Tears welled up in Reg's eyes once again. I should have stopped, but I didn't.

"You told me that you carry around the thought of her like a weight, and you feel it every day, crushing you. You told me that when you drink is the only time that weight lightens, and that's why you think you'll probably end up drinking yourself to death. You told me that not a day passes that you don't wonder what happened to her. To her soul."

Now the tears were streaming down his face. He wasn't sobbing this time. He was just letting them fall, silently, leaving streaks on his cheeks. And he didn't take his eyes from mine.

"I can't promise you what lies beyond those gates. The honest truth is that I have no idea. But if you ever want to see your sister again," I sucked in a breath before I pushed out the last sentence, "then she's waiting for you back there."

Reg leapt down from the throne and pulled me into another tight embrace — but this time it was not an expression of relief. No, it was something else. Gratitude. Then he wordlessly looked to Narissa, and he took her hand.

I did not follow. I looked back at Freya for only a brief moment before running back to my office, hoping that neither woman had seen me begin to cry.

§

When I heard the door to my office open and close, I didn't bother to look up. Narissa had a habit of entering uninvited, so it was nothing new.

"What do you want this time?"

"No need to be testy. I'm only apologizing," said a voice that was certainly not Narissa's. I looked up in alarm and saw Freya standing before me in her usual purple gown and flower crown.

"What are you doing here?" I demanded.

"I told you. I'm apologizing. Not because I think I did anything wrong," she added abruptly, "But because I know it was hard for you, and I'm sorry about that. I really don't have any control over who you argue in front of. Really. I don't get to choose who dies. But I did make the choice to throw you in unprepared."

"You were trying," I hissed, "to make me quit."

She shrugged. "I thought you might," she said as nonchalantly as though she were discussing changes in the NASDAQ.

"You wanted me to kill myself," I accused.

"I wouldn't go that —"

"The way I see it, you attempted murder!" I stood, nearly knocking my chair back.

"Murder?" she gasped overdramatically, then threw her head back with a hearty laugh. "I gave you a little push! There's nothing wrong with that. I do it all the time."

"And because you do it all the time, it's okay?"

Freya blinked. "Yes," she said. "Obviously."

"I don't get how you could..." I struggled for the right words, "I don't get how you can do something like this. You're *life*. And yet you were the one trying to convince *me* to die? It doesn't make sense. It's...it's counter to your nature!" I thought perhaps I'd given her something to think about there, but she only smiled and shook her head, sitting on my desk like Narissa often did.

"You're right. It is counter to my nature to try and convince you to go to What Come Next. But you were taking too many souls away from me. It pained me to make you consider death — it physically pained me." Her eyes flicked away from me and for a moment I could have sworn she was embarrassed. "It was a sacrifice I needed to make for the many."

I eyed her silently but said nothing. She turned back to face me and I realized I was seeing her eyes up close for the first time. They were gold, and they flashed when she spoke, like a little flame flickered behind them.

"You think you're so smart," she shook her head fondly, the shadow of a grin on her face, "and you are, for a human. But the truth is, you'll never be like us."

"Yes, and I'd never want to be. I don't really think being a pompous deity suits me."

Again, she laughed. "I'm sorry you're so...put off by us. Really, I am. But it's hard not to be 'pompous' as you say when you *are,* in fact, a deity. It's just par for the course."

"Well it's not exactly the best way to make friends."

She gave me a pitying look. "Did you ever think I was trying to make friends with you, Dev?"

I opened my mouth to speak, then closed it abruptly. I suppose I had always thought of us as natural enemies, but something about her...the way she existed in the world...it was like she *wanted* me to like her. I sensed it. And despite everything, I still did.

"I think perhaps," I began, eyeing her coolly, "you might like to be able to relate with a human for a change. And I'm simply letting you know that you're doing a bad job. You — both of you — are arrogant, entitled, and insensitive, and I think —"

"Then why are you still here?" Freya cut me off.

"What?"

"If you don't like us, then why are you still here?"

"I never said I didn't like you." And that was true. Despite how much they irritated me, I found both entities...charming, in their own unique way.

"I *am* sorry," Freya repeated. "And I suppose I *would* like to be a little more...approachable to humans."

"Well you and Narissa both could use some lessons." I sat back down to give my statement a sense of finality, looking back to my work. Freya seemed to take the hint, standing up, but before I knew what I was doing I grabbed her hand to stop her.

"I'm sorry too," I blurted out. "You were only doing your job just like I was doing mine. I see that now. On a...on a cosmic scale, I suppose...you were only doing what's right."

Freya smiled, gently patting my hand and placing it back on my desk.

"So were you," she murmured, and with that she walked out.

§

I argued 2,567 cases. Some of them I remember as clearly as if I'd only just stepped out of the courtroom. Others I have no recollection of at all. I wish I could say I was counting the days, waiting for the moment that I would be free. But I wasn't. I grew comfortable. I even began to feel happy. I began to feel a warmth blossom between Narissa and I, between Freya and I, between the three of us. Perhaps this is the kind of bond they form with each of the lawyers that pass through the In Between, but I like to flatter myself and think that I was special.

Then one day Narissa appeared in my office and I could tell something was different. She didn't have her trademark confidence about her. She always looked deathly, but for the first time since I'd met her, she looked sad. She didn't say anything. She just waved a hand indicating that I should follow her, and I did so without question. I knew where we were going. She stopped in front of the wrought-iron gates, stone pillars towering high above us.

I glanced at her, then up at the gates in front of me, and I knew she didn't want to say it herself: one hundred years had passed. One hundred years and one day.

"It's been a pleasure working with you," I finally said.

"Has it?" she asked without looking at me, eyes trained forward at the gate.

"Absolutely not."

"Leave it to a lawyer to lie that convincingly."

"It's what I do best."

"Funny. For the most part I've only ever heard you tell the truth."

"Well, I'm pretty damn good at that too."

She waited for me to step towards the gates but I didn't. She continued staring forward at them.

"I lied," she murmured.

"What?"

"I told you that some of my lawyers finished their term. I lied. None of them ever have. They've all quit. Every single one. Hell, even the guy who had to convince his own mother was a lie. I tell that to everyone just to scare them a little. Truth is, most don't get more than a few years in. You've been my most loyal by a long shot."

I stared at her, her stony face still directed at the gate. "Why are you telling me this?" I asked.

"Because if you give in to temptation, if you walk through those doors, I'm telling you that I get it. You've held out longer than any of the rest. You can go now. You can be free. If that's what you want." She took a long breath. "You can rest."

I glanced back at the gates, and for a long moment I listened to their song. I stood next to death herself, and I listened to the gentle call of the In Between. Then I spoke.

"You know what I really want, Narissa?"

"What?"

"I want to stay here and work with you. Forever." I don't believe she was capable of crying, but I could have sworn I saw her eyes brim with tears.

"You can't do that," she murmured. "The cycle must continue. Humans are transient. Only gods are forever. You are not a god, Dev, much as you might like to think you are."

"But you could make me one," I pressed. "You have that power, don't you? You could keep me here forever. And you want to."

Narissa still refused to look at me. "You wouldn't like that."

"How do you know?"

"Some humans envy gods..." she stared longingly at the glimmering gates, "but all gods envy humans."

It occurred to me for the first time that the gentle call I heard for the past hundred years...she must hear it too. A lullaby, calling her to sleep. And she cannot sleep. She cannot rest. And yet, after having been through so much with her, I still wanted to stay by her side instead of getting the rest for which I was so painfully overdue.

"Couldn't you let me be the judge of that? For once in one hundred years, can't you let *me* be the judge?" She shook her head.

"I couldn't let you choose not to come here. And I can't let you choose to stay. But!" she swiveled abruptly, doffing her maudlin airs in favor of her usual brusqueness, "you do still get a choice. You may go through those gates, or you may return to your life. For the first time, the choice is really, truly yours."

Well, I'm here, writing this to you, and not gallivanting off in What Come Next, so I suppose you can surmise what I chose. The truth is, during these hundred years, I almost lost myself in this job. Almost. I almost gave myself up to Narissa, to Freya. But not a day passed that I didn't think of my clients. They would all pass through this place. Everyone does. But it is my duty to ensure that before that time, they see justice. And even after all this time, I cannot let go of that. Because everyone — and I mean everyone — deserves a defense.

As soon as I seal this envelope and place it on your desk — my old office should be just to the left of yours, if you want to take a peek — Narissa will ferry me back. Something she's never done before. I will wake up at around ten in the morning. I will clean up the red wine stain on my nice new carpet. I will hear the news of Reg's death, and I'll attend the funeral. And I will go back to work.

The job's not too hard, really. Just remind yourself why you're doing it. Don't let Narissa get you down, and don't let Freya get under your skin. They truly do mean well.

I'm sure you'll do fine. If you make it through the night, come find me when you wake up. I'd love to have a chat. And if you don't, well, I'm sure you must have given yourself a damn good argument.

Sincerely,

Your predecessor,
Dev Fielding, Esq.

A Tea Party

I was not expecting a visitor, but when I opened my eyes to see it standing at the foot of my bed, limbs stretched out like saltwater taffy, eyes glowing like two distant stars, distorted as though I were seeing it through foggy glasses, it seemed like the most natural thing in the world.

It did not speak to me, and I could hear its silence clearly. It lifted its inky black tendrils and glided towards the door. I threw on my robe, stepped into my slippers, and followed. That's what it wanted, after all. I could tell.

It guided me down labyrinthine streets, the same streets I walked every day. But they seemed different now that the creature was here. Brighter, lit by a moon that wasn't there. The gravel crunched under the weight of my feet, but the creature moved silently. With each footfall I could hear the absence of a step. And that seemed right to me. Why would it make any noise? It didn't weigh anything. I knew this.

The streets were empty, and I could tell this was because the creature did not want to be seen. It was very shy. Strange to see these serpentine streets so abandoned, but this was to be private. Everyone else was sleeping, so we meandered down the winding alleys completely alone. My instincts told me to be afraid, but somehow the fear didn't come. I felt safe against my better judgment, as though I knew the creature would let no harm come to me.

It came to a stop at a cafe, wooden sign creaking ever so slightly in the wind. The cafe was closed, but still a little table stood by the door, inviting us to sit and share a cup of tea. The table was there because the creature was there. I knew this. The creature pulled out a chair for me, and I thanked it. They were the first words I'd spoken to it aloud. It bent its long neck and its head bobbed in acknowledgment. When it moved, the line between the creature and the rest of the world began to blur. It sat across from me and poured me a cup of tea. Jasmine.

"Why did you bring me here?" I asked, breathing in the sweet steam.

I am lonely, it told me. It did not speak. But it told me. *I would like a friend.*

"I can't be your friend," I said apologetically, sipping my tea.

I know, it answered without answering, *but I can pretend.*

And we spent the night that way, me sipping my tea and prattling on, the creature speaking to me without speaking at all.

The next morning I awoke and I had no question in my mind that it had all been real. On my tongue I could still taste the jasmine tea.

Acknowledgements

Big shoutout to the members of the Silent Notetakers Writers' Collective who gave me feedback on these stories: Grace Griego, Elliott Yordy, Shaoni C. White, Yarrow Syskine, and Alexander Sheldon. Thank you also to the people who agreed to write some nice things about this silly little book of mine: H.R. Owen, Jeremy Enfinger, Grace Griego, Sean McLachlan, and Shaoni C. White. Thanks to Sora James and Sean McLachlan who helped me so much in navigating the publishing world. And I'm so grateful to the original publication venues that were kind enough to first share my work with the world: *Sci-Fi Lampoon, Orion's Beau, Radon Journal, The Storage Papers,* and *The Ensemble Arts Exchange.*

About the Author

Alex Kingsley (they/them) is a writer, comedian, and game designer. They graduated from Swarthmore College with High Honors and are a part of SFWA. They are a co-founder of new media company Strong Branch Productions, where they write and direct science-fiction comedy podcast *The Stench of Adventure* and edit weird fiction anthology show *Tales From The Radiator* . Their sci-fi play "The Bearer of Bad News" was produced by the Annenberg Foundation. In addition to their fiction, their non-fiction has appeared in *Interstellar Flight Press, Ancillary Review of Books*, and more. Alex's tabletop games can be found at alexyquest.itch.io, and their dramatic catalog can be found on the New Play Exchange.

For more information, visit alexkingsley.org
Twitter: @alexyquest
Mastodon: alexyquest.podvibes.co
Instagram: hitchhikersguidetothealexy

Printed in the USA
CPSIA information can be obtained
at www.ICGtesting.com
LVHW011240220624
783589LV00010BA/236